DEMON STALKERS

STALKERS

PrEy

Coming soon

DEMON STALKERS: TORMENT
DEMON STALKERS: VENGEANCE

DEMON STALKERS

PREY

Douglas Hill

MACMILLAN CHILDREN'S BOOKS

First published 2008 by Macmillan Children's Books
a division of Macmillan Publishers Limited
20 New Wharf Road, London N1 9RR
Basingstoke and Oxford
Associated companies throughout the world
www.panmacmillan.com

ISBN 978-0-330-45214-4

1 3 5 7 9 8 6 4 2

A CIP catalogue record for this book is available from
the British Library.

Typeset by Intype Libra Limited
Printed and bound in the UK by CPI Mackays, Chatham ME5 8TD

In memory of Mackenzie Ray Mourne –
barman, factory worker, lecturer, journalist,
freelance writer, editor,
father and grandfather

1

The cracked mirror stopped me in my tracks.

It reminded me of the mirror I saw on the night when the ordinary desperate life I was living came to an end. When I was . . . changed.

People say that a broken mirror is bad luck, but they're wrong. Luck, good or bad, isn't something you can bring on or keep away. It just happens, whatever you do, like rainfall or nightfall. It's a part of life.

Part of my life, anyway.

But this mirror, in a dirty shop window, turned out to be good luck. When I stopped to look, it showed a twitch of movement on the street behind me. A dark shape, pulling back into shadow.

Without turning I took out the knife. The October afternoon gloom was making the blade glimmer a little, but in its usual silvery way, not golden. So the shape behind me could just be an ordinary person, nothing to do with me at all.

But it was more likely to be something else, just not close enough to make the knife react.

I thought about circling around and coming up behind it, but that would be risky until I knew more about it. As all wild animals and street kids know, when in doubt it's usually better to run.

I put the knife away, yanked open the shop door and stepped in. I'd been in that place before, because it sold old books and other bits and pieces to do with magic and the supernatural and so on. It was also dingy, dusty and cluttered, on a slow downward slide to being just another junk shop.

'What d'*you* want, boy?' The owner was bulky, tough-looking and loud-voiced, and didn't see me as likely to buy anything. 'I'm closing!'

'Good,' I said, slamming the door behind me and turning the key in the lock.

'Here!' the owner growled. 'What's your game? Get out!'

He came at me, beefy hands reaching. But for all his noise his bulk was mostly loose fat, and he moved in slow-mo. I swerved around his lunge, leaving a foot trailing, and when he tripped I added a push that sent him headlong into a free-standing bookcase.

He and the shelves crashed to the floor, books and curses flying everywhere, and I leaped past the tattered curtain across the doorway at the back of the shop. It led to a back room holding more heaps of books and fortune-telling junk, along with a chair and a kettle and a tiny TV. It also had a window, which didn't squeak too loudly when I forced it open.

Slipping through, I dropped down into a small, badly paved area with dustbins that didn't smell much worse than the shop had. It was one of many fenced-off areas – they couldn't be called gardens – behind that row of shops and crumbling old houses. I slid through a handy hole in a fence, hopped over the next.

Behind me I heard a crash of breaking glass. I wondered if the shop owner would have the sense to stay out of the way.

Several more fences brought me to a spot with a few straggly bushes. I used their cover to take a quick look back, just in time to see whatever it was come up on to a fence some distance behind me. A smooth movement, but not springy like an athlete or a cat. More like slithery.

I didn't look at it directly, since it might have felt my eyes on it. Even ordinary people can tell when they're being watched. But I saw its long crouching shape, all in black, on the fence. I felt a faint edge of the chill that such creatures always bring with them. And I noticed the oval eyes that seemed to glow faintly in the twilight as it stared around, searching.

Right, I thought. No question now what it was. But

there'd be better places to face it than littered yards behind houses, at night – if I was going to have to face it at all. So when it moved again I moved too, finding another gap in another half-collapsed fence. And leaping away just in time, as a mouthful of long sharp teeth clashed where my leg had been.

It was a big heavy-shouldered dog, trained to attack without barking or even growling. Luckily, it was held by a sturdy rope that kept its teeth away from me.

Edging sideways, I drew the knife again, which was starting to glow gold now that the dark slithery shape was closer.

Then I whisked around behind the dog, sliced through the rope and was over the next fence before the dog realized it was free.

One more fence, then a higher wall of old weather-worn brick. I'd got good at climbing over the years, and old brick offers lots of fingerholds and toeholds. So I was up and over in a flash.

Somewhere behind me I heard a gargling shriek of pain and fury. 'Good dog,' I whispered.

A narrow passage between two houses showed the way to a street, and I sprinted flat out with the knife lighting my way. So I still had the knife in my hand when I burst out on to the street, busy with people and cars and lights coming on.

And two big policemen in my way.

But of course they didn't – couldn't – see the knife.

'What's the rush, sonny?' one asked.

'Getting home,' I said, sheathing the knife. 'I'm late.'

'Where's home?' the other asked.

I gave them a non-existent address, along with a wide-eyed, anxious, innocent look.

'What were you doing in there?' the second one growled, nodding towards the dark passageway.

'I thought it might be a short cut,' I said. 'But it wasn't.'

The first one grunted. 'Let's have a look at you, then.'

I'd had the standard stop-and-search more times than I could count. It was because I look like the kind of kid who might be carrying drugs or burglar tools or some sort of weapon. But they've never found anything. I didn't usually carry much at all, except a bit of cash when I had some. And the knife.

One of the cops actually pushed its sheath aside as he was prodding around my waist, but didn't notice a thing. And since my pockets were empty, they finally sent me on my way with a suspicious glower.

They would have seen what was stalking me, though, if it had got past the dog. So maybe their presence helped to hold it back. Anyway, I saw no sign of it behind me, and the knife's gleam was pure silver again as I ran all the way home.

I'd been staying in a small two-storey house on one of the city's back streets where shabby houses huddle together in terraces. Usually with broken furniture or leaking bags of rubbish decorating the pavement. But when you live more or less in the shadows, on the wrong side of whatever line there is, you don't much care what your home looks like.

If where you live has a roof and walls, you call that a blessing. And if you're *safe* there, it's perfect.

With the front door firmly closed behind me, I stood in the hall for a moment, enjoying the relief, glancing at the old cloudy mirror in the hall. I always knew I wasn't going to see even the tiniest hint of a change. But I always hoped . . .

The image was the same as ever. A lean dark-eyed youth in frayed jeans and a faded jacket. With black hair that needed cutting and a cheekbony face that sometimes let me get away with pretending to be eighteen.

But I wasn't. I was fourteen.

I'd been fourteen for years.

2

Outside, a wind was getting up, joined by a burst of rain. But it wasn't the weather that made me shiver. It was the memories, rising up as always when something has come to hunt me, as clear and nightmarish as if it had been only the day before.

I turned towards the stairs, heading up to my small room on the upper floor of the house. It held only a narrow mattress on the floor, a small cardboard box for the few spare clothes and other bits that I owned, and one or two beat-up old books. Still miles better than some places I've lived.

As I dropped on to the mattress, the single bulb hanging from the ceiling swayed, making the shadows in the corners move. But I paid no attention. I wasn't even thinking about the slithery shadow that I'd run from.

As so often before, I was locked into the full-colour non-stop horror show of the memories . . .

It was October back then, too, and it had been raining for days, on either side of my fourteenth birthday. I had a flimsy shelter, bits of boards and plastic bags, on a patch of waste ground. But after the wind knocked it over for the tenth time, I left it and wandered out to the edge of town, looking for a disused shed or something.

I knew there were probably better places to sleep rough on the streets than that grimy east-coast town. But I'd been born there, and knew every inch of it. Another place might be warmer, but I wouldn't know my way around. And that was more important.

By then I'd been on my own for two years. It hadn't been that much different from how I'd lived for as long as I could remember. I never knew my dad, and my mum was more interested in booze than in me. Home was a series of cheap dirty rooms, where I invented games that could be played with empty bottles and tried to ignore being hungry.

When mum died of a ruined liver, official strangers wanted to put me into a children's 'home' that looked like a jail. I wasn't about to swap my freedom for their rules, and I'd already learned some survival lessons, the hard way. So I took off – into that shadowy outcast world that ordinary people try not to see.

I got along well enough, on the streets, so I was

still fairly healthy and not too unhappy on that particular rainy October night when I was looking for a new shelter. When, on the edge of town, I found a deserted building on an abandoned railway line.

It had probably been both ticket office and waiting room – now with smashed windows, a door sagging half open and holes in its thin walls. But it had a roof, and it was a lot better than huddling under plastic bags.

As I slid in through the door, I was grinning at my good luck, thinking that if the place was isolated enough I might make it my home through the winter.

I've wished every day since that I'd never seen the place, that I'd taken my chances with sleeping in a ditch under a bush.

It was nearly pitch black inside, so I crept forward slowly, hands held out to keep me from walking into something. It had all the usual smells of an old disused building – mildew and rotten wood, mouse droppings and cat spray. And the sewer stink that told me other homeless people had passed through.

Then I noticed another faint smell, totally out of place. Like perfume, sweet and musky.

That was when the light came on.

It wasn't a bulb or any kind of electric light. It was as if the cobwebby ceiling itself had begun to glow.

9

And I would have jumped with the sudden shock of it. But I couldn't move.

In the instant when the light came on, something that felt like cold rubbery slime wrapped itself around me, head to foot.

It was a powerful grip, so that I couldn't twitch a finger or open my mouth or move an eyelid. Yet it was clear, so that I could see through it with only a little blurring. And, just as impossibly, despite its grip I could breathe normally.

So I breathed, as much as terror allowed – until terror swelled into near-panic.

Across the empty space of the ticket office a shape came drifting silently towards me. A man-sized shiny-purple thing, with wide sweeping wings and claws that were bright red as if they'd been dipped in blood.

But then my vision cleared a little and I realized with total amazement that it wasn't a horror-creature at all.

It was a woman with huge green eyes, pale skin and red-gold hair that swirled down over her shoulders. She was wearing a long purple dress made of some shiny material, with wide wrist-length sleeves that had looked like wings when she spread her arms. And her long fingernails, painted scarlet, did look a lot like claws.

It might have seemed funny, that I'd mistaken her for a monster. But she had terrifyingly drifted towards me through the air, just above the floor. And I was still held tight by the gluey invisible slime.

All that was a long way from being funny.

And then it got worse.

'Can you be one of them?' the woman murmured. Her voice was shaking slightly, but I couldn't tell if it was anger or fear. 'Wearing the shape of a dirty little Powerless boy?'

I had no idea what she was talking about, and couldn't speak anyway. I just stared at her in sheer terror. Which got worse when she moved her hand in an odd gesture in front of my face.

'Now you can speak,' she said. 'Tell me who you are.'

I gasped and panted, realizing that my face had been freed from the slime. But I managed nothing more than a choked whimper.

'I have no time for your silence,' she snapped. 'Speak. Tell me your name.'

Despite my terror, I found a small scrap of nerve. Enough to make me feel that I really didn't want to whimper again.

'W-Walker,' I said, fighting to control my voice. 'Nick Walker.'

'Walker?' Her eyes flashed. 'A good name for a

stray child . . . Or are you something else, looking for me?'

'No!' I said. 'I was looking for a place to sleep. I don't know anything about you.'

'I am Manta,' she said. 'And if that is a disguise, it is very imaginative.'

She seemed to murmur to herself for a moment, words I couldn't catch, then moved both her hands in another odd gesture. The grip of the invisible slime vanished from around me.

And as I swayed, a knife appeared from nowhere in her hand.

It had a black, ridged hilt and about eight inches of double-edged blade that weirdly seemed to be glowing, bright silver. I stared at it, held as still by fright as I'd been by the slime, trying to keep my legs and my bladder from giving way.

But the woman, Manta, just studied the knife, nodding. 'Very well, Nick Walker. You are unlikely to be wearing a disguise that can resist both my sight and this blade. So you must be what you say you are.' She peered intently at me for a long moment. 'You may also be just what I need.'

Still gripping the knife, she raised her other hand, which was suddenly holding a book that also came from nowhere. An old, thick book with rough-edged pages and a leather cover. She seemed to be looking for something in it, turning pages with the knife-point, muttering.

I tried taking a stealthy step back. But my feet wouldn't lift from the floor, as if she had left some of the invisible gluey slime on the soles of my shoes.

'Please,' I begged. 'Please let me go. I can't be what you need.' My voice trembled like the rest of me. 'I can't do anything for you.'

Manta looked up at me. 'Not so. I have looked within you, into your mind and nature, and I have seen many qualities. You are capable of much more than you think, Nick Walker. And I must now help you stay alive, so you may find and use those qualities.'

She was no longer holding the knife. In her hand instead was a flat disc with a symbol on it – curved overlapping shapes, inky-black. Her fingers flickered, the disc went suddenly blank, and I felt an odd warmth in the hollow of my throat.

And in a bit of broken mirror on the wall behind Manta, I saw the symbol, the overlapping black shapes. On the very skin of my throat, like a brand or tattoo.

I've seen it happen often, since then, when an ordinary person gets a clear sight of that power – magic, sorcery, witchcraft, whatever. The mind freezes, in a *way – refusing to believe it but at the same time knowing that it did happen and it's absolutely soul-blastingly terrifying . . . Some people just go numb and dazed, some have hysterics, a few actually go insane.*

I did the numb and dazed thing for a while, so I was only half aware that Manta was peering at the book again, murmuring. But what she said at last got through to me, and pumped up my terror level another notch.

'By the power of the Mark,' she chanted, 'let this work be fixed and forever. By the Mark of Change-lessness, let him be as he is. Let him be as he is. Let him be as he is . . .'

I felt a sickening wrenching twisting quiver inside every bit of me, flesh and bone and blood. Then she sighed, sounding weary, and the book vanished from her hand.

'What have you done to me?' I gasped.

A shadow of sadness darkened her eyes. 'I did what had to be done. Listen now, and learn.' Her eyes went bright again. 'There is a group, sometimes called the Cartel, powerful sorcerers and their . . . creatures. Dedicated to evil – to greed and corruption – to enlarging their power in both sorcery and the Power-less world. I have fought them however I could for years, and they in turn have pursued me.'

14

I might have asked many questions. But I asked the only one that my dazed, appalled mind could manage.

'Why?' I croaked.

Her eyes grew haunted. 'I am their enemy because they took . . . something from me, my most treasured possession, now perhaps lost to me forever. So I seek vengeance. I will harass and thwart and damage them however I can, for as long as I live.'

I might have felt sorry for her, if she hadn't terrified me and done something magical to me. And if she hadn't then started looking even more eerie and wild.

'I also kill them when I can,' she breathed, and my skin crawled. 'Not by my own hand, since that would warp and corrupt my powers, but with other weapons that I have shaped.' Her eyes flared. 'As I have now shaped you.'

I said nothing, not understanding, not wanting to. Then I gasped – as the cold, ridged hilt of her knife magically appeared in my hand, and its dark-metal sheath attached itself to my belt.

And I saw that the blade's silvery glow had become a rich, dazzling gold.

'The blade turns golden when one of them is near,' she whispered. 'Its brightness now says the danger is very close. So I must flee – and you must confront it.'

3

Whatever held my feet to the floor was also the only thing still keeping me upright. 'Me?' I gasped. 'No! I can't . . . !'

'I cannot ever spill blood, so I *must* hope that you will.' Her eyes held the tinge of sadness again. 'I wish I could make you invincible – but that too is beyond me. This is the best I can do for you in the time I have.'

As she spoke the light around me seemed to dim slightly, and the air grew colder. Then my nerves fizzed with new shock when another voice behind me began to laugh, harsh and ugly. And in the cracked mirror I saw someone, half hidden in shadow, standing in the doorway.

'Tell him more, Manta.' The voice from the shadows was as nasty as the laugh. 'Tell how your victories against us are few and trivial. Tell how you endlessly flee our wrath, coming now to cower in this rural misery.'

Manta's eyes blazed. 'I do not cower,' she snarled.

More nasty laughter, as the someone stepped forward. And I nearly screamed.

In the light I saw an impossible creature – a human shape, squat and muscular, but covered in matted hair. With a beast's sharp muzzle and pointed ears, a beast's lethal fangs and claws.

'I am Harne,' the monster growled, its cruel eyes glittering, 'and you should cower. Especially when my masters have shielded me against your witchery.' He laughed again. 'They would be amazed to see you lurking here with one of the Powerless. A skinny feeble boy, at that.'

'Not so feeble now,' Manta snapped.

The beast-man snorted. 'I see your little mark on him, and the blade he can barely hold. Do you think that will protect him? Do you imagine, witch, that will let him protect you?'

And he opened his fanged beast-mouth and sprang at her.

But Manta somehow suddenly moved herself away, towards the window.

And the magic that had held my feet to the floor sent me lurching forward, into the path of the beast.

I did scream, then, as one of his clawed hands grabbed me. Pain flared through me as the claws sank deep into my right shoulder. The knife dropped from my less-used right hand, made totally useless by the agony in my shoulder.

On the edge of my vision I saw that the window was open and Manta was gone. But she must still have been near, aware of what was happening. For as I struggled to keep the monster's jaws from my throat, the knife flew up into my stronger – left – hand.

Weirdly, that magical help was just what I needed. I'd fought my way out of many bad times on the streets, making up for a lack of bulk with speed and balance and a hard-won ability to keep cool and avoid panic. Now the knife in my hand gave me something else to fight with.

As his fangs came closer I swung it at him, and he jerked his head away from the golden blade. Furiously I slashed at him again as he tried to grab my left wrist, and the blade sliced across his forearm.

His blood spurted, and he jerked back with a hoarse cry. Spurred on by that, I kept wildly slashing.

And one sweep of the golden blade sliced smoothly across the monster's throat and cut him a second mouth as wide as the first.

More blood burst from that wound, dark and thick as tar. The claws tore away from my shoulder as the monster fell. As he writhed and died, his body began to collapse and shrink. And that new horror, along *with the pain, finished me off. I blacked out, collapsing beside what was left of him.*

When I came to, a wet grey dawn had replaced the magical light. And everything around me also looked perfectly normal. Which was the weirdest thing of all.

The monster had shrivelled away to nothing, not even a drop of its tarry blood left on the floor. And Manta was long gone as well. I was totally alone.

And I was no longer hurt and bleeding, not feeling even the smallest twinge of pain.

Even so, I knew beyond all doubt that it had all been real, not a sick weird nightmare. I really had been fighting for my life against a monstrous enemy.

I knew because although my right shoulder didn't have a mark on it, the right sleeve of my jacket and the shirt under it were ripped to bits.

And my left hand was still holding the knife, now glowing a peaceful silver.

So my new life began, as it was to go on. Through just about every moment in the years since that night, I kept the knife with me. Just as I also still had the dark shape of Manta's mark on my throat. Indelibly.

And through all that time, I didn't change.

I stayed fourteen, on the outside. I changed my clothes but nothing else. I didn't grow even a millimetre taller than I was then. I never gained or lost weight, no matter how or what I ate. My hair and nails never grew, and if I tried cutting them – even if I shaved my head – in a few minutes they would all be back to the way they'd been before.

I also never got sick, which is something. If I'd had a cold when I met Manta, I'd probably have been sniffling ever since. But I never have. Which has been a blessing for someone who's homeless.

And though I could get hurt, like anyone, and feel pain – as I learned in the fight with Harne the beast-man – the damage and the pain have always just *disappeared*, in minutes.

So some might think that what Manta did to me was a real favour. And she *had* given me the knife as well.

I didn't like it much. I've never thought of it as *my* knife. It has sometimes sickened me a bit. But I never forgot how much I needed it when I faced Harne, and how often it has helped me survive since. When its golden glow has warned me of some new prowling horror sent by the evil that Manta called the Cartel.

Besides that, the blade has never lost its sharpness and may even be unbreakable, though I've never risked any drastic tests. And of course it's usefully invisible to the Powerless.

Above all, having a magical weapon against the stalkers has given me something special. Not any kind of actual power: the knife didn't have that kind of magic.

But it has given me a bit of confidence when I needed it. Maybe I wouldn't have survived without that either.

All the same, even with being changeless, even with the knife, I was still human. I knew I'd die some day, and could be killed any time. And others knew as well.

Which was where the magic that Manta put on me stopped being a blessing and became a curse.

The dark power of the Cartel would have shown them who killed their creature, Harne, that night. And would have shown them what Manta had made of me. They hadn't forgotten, and never would.

I knew that they'd keep hunting me till they finished me.

4

The demon stalkers, I've since learned, are all part human, part monster. Specially bred or formed by the Cartel's magic – dangerous, savage, deadly creatures. So in the first year or two I survived mostly by dumb luck. I made one hunter chase me on to a busy motorway where a truck got him. I helped another fall off a railway bridge with a train coming. Like that.

And as their hunters died, the Cartel became more determined to kill me.

When I first realized that I'd go on being a target for evil and vengeful sorcerers, I wanted to find Manta and somehow force her to make me normal again and use her magic to hide me. Some hope. I had no chance of finding a powerful witch who lived in permanent hiding.

And that was another thing she'd done to me. I discovered, later, that all the magical people and creatures, good or evil, in this island country are permanently unable to cross salt water. Their powers are linked with the mystic essence of the land, or something like that. They can't leave. And neither could I.

So I couldn't get a job on a freighter and vanish to America or Australia. I was stuck in this country, where the Cartel was.

But at least, along the way, I learned some useful things. Survival skills, adding to the ones I'd started learning as a little kid. I became good at running and climbing and staying out of sight. When I had to stand and fight, I learned to be quick and vicious and totally committed, no holding back. And I grew able to bear a lot of pain and fear without falling apart and losing control.

I already knew, from childhood, how to bear hunger and cold. And loneliness.

Weirdly, I was *advised* to learn the skills I've picked up. By Manta. She invaded my dreams, or nightmares, many times since that terrible night when I met her. But in a way the first dream, a week or so after that night, was the worst.

'I see that I was right about you, Nick Walker,' her dream-image told me. She seemed to be in a glowing cavern, wearing a different dress, her hair wild, her eyes wilder. 'That there is more to you than even *you* realize. You did remarkably well against Harne. Now you must continue to do well.'

23

In the dream her image drifted closer, her eyes luminous and intent.

'You have been a wanderer, a rootless drifter, and so you will continue. But now, also, you must be always on your guard. You must learn to use what I have given you, along with your own courage and intelligence. You must learn to face them and to fight them . . . But above all you must stay alive, you must *survive*.'

The image came even closer, so that I saw only the blazing green of her eyes.

'Evil *can* be fought, victories can be won against it. And *must* be, so that it does not gain the total mastery that it seeks . . .'

The dream faded, and I woke up. And I stayed awake the rest of the night, in the ruined, rat-infested barn where I was staying at the time. Feeling scared, but also filled with new rage against her for having drafted me into her magical war against the Cartel.

But before long I saw the sense in some of what she'd said, and began to learn what I needed to know.

And from then on, until very recently, I've been more or less what that dream said I had to be. A wanderer, a drifter – but never aimless. A wanderer with a purpose.

To stay alive, despite the hunters. To fight back, when and how I could.

And now there was a new hunter. A slithery, glowing-eyed one. Who was probably more than annoyed, after meeting that dog.

With that thought, as if on cue to scare me rigid, I heard the stairs creak outside my door. And I was on my feet, the knife ready in my hand, crouched by the open window in case I needed to run, when the door was pushed slowly open.

Knuckles tapped lightly on its panel. 'You there, Nick?'

Paddy. The owner of the house. He and his partner, Julia, lived on the ground floor, which they'd fixed up very nicely. Julia was a thin and slightly faded blonde, with the sort of shadowed eyes and nerviness that I've seen in ex-junkies. Or maybe she was just nervous of me. She definitely tended to stay out of my way.

I didn't know all that much about either of them. Paddy never liked to talk about himself, and Julia didn't talk to me much about anything. Still, Paddy was just about the only real friend I'd ever had. And the two of them were the only people I knew who called me by my first name.

On the streets I'm just Walker. Like Manta, the street people thought it was funny for a young homeless drifter to have such a suitable name. So it was a nice change when Paddy called me Nick. Though I liked it best when, now and then, in the easy way of this city, he called me 'son'.

He looked round the door, then came all the way in. He was of average height and sturdy, with curly ginger hair going thin on top, a short ginger beard with some grey in it, blue eyes that usually twinkled under bushy brows. Though just then they were looking worried.

'You're being hunted again,' he said in his gruff voice.

It wasn't a question, but I shrugged and nodded. 'Something sneaky and snaky. I didn't wait around to get a good look.'

Paddy nodded. He'd learned quite a bit about me and my life. I'd told him some of it – but he also picked things up. He was a psychic, with a lot of ESP that could sense all sorts of different things around him. Including a bit of what's going on inside people's heads.

But though he was fairly powerful, no one would've known from the way he lived. He was sharp and experienced and knew a lot, and he could probably have made a good living. Especially if he used his powers. But he didn't, because he thought it would be dishonest and cruel.

Anyway, he said, people like him with a good bit of magical power, of any sort, often drew the attention of the Cartel. And then those people either got recruited or they disappeared.

So Paddy worked part-time for a mental-health charity, did the psychic stuff only for friends and kept his head down.

He turned slowly all the way around, head tilted as if listening. 'Whatever's after you, it's not near here, as far as I can tell. But stay close for a few days. I'll keep a lookout.'

That suited me fine, since I had nowhere I needed to go in a hurry. And I was in no rush to run into those glowing eyes again.

5

Anyway, Paddy's place was safer than most places. His ESP would warn him about any trouble coming, and he had some kind of magical protection around the house, put there by a mage he knew. He also wore a personal-protection amulet, probably made by the same mage. And I knew how well that worked.

It was how we met. On a back street in a humid July twilight, where three older teenage thugs with knives were furious that I didn't have a mobile or anything else worth stealing. When Paddy came along, I was reaching for the knife at my hip.

I didn't want to use it on ordinary people, whom the magic people call the Powerless. But I didn't want to be stabbed either.

Paddy didn't pause or even blink, just kept walking towards us. 'That's enough, boys,' he said. 'On your way now.'

'On *your* way, old man!' one thug snarled, and struck at Paddy with his blade.

But it never landed. A blaze of dazzling white light burst from Paddy's chest – from the amulet that he wears inside his shirt. It blocked the attack and wrenched the knife out of the thug's hand, probably spraining a few fingers. And all three yelped, stared in horror, then turned and ran.

'Never liked muggers,' Paddy said, gruff but smiling. 'You can put your knife away now.'

I did so, realizing that he could see it because he was magical, wondering edgily what else he was. Meanwhile, he was looking me over, still smiling.

'I live nearby,' he said, 'with a lady who's also been a waif and stray in her time, and who is a fair cook. There'll be supper enough for you too, if you like.'

He'd come to my rescue, I was hugely curious about him, and I'd been sleeping in doorways and hadn't eaten all day. So I went with him, got a wan smile and hot shepherd's pie from Julia, and stayed the night. And stayed, and stayed – in the closest thing to a home I'd had for years.

Not that I ever hoped to have a permanent home. People around me – neighbours, shopkeepers, whoever – would soon start wondering about a fourteen-year-old who never grew or changed. But it meant a lot to me, to be safe and welcome in that house.

It was good for me in other ways too, because Paddy taught me a lot. Especially about the enemy, the Cartel.

'Remember, Nick,' he told me once, early on, 'that besides the magic that makes you changeless, and your own nerve and all that, there's something else that has kept you alive. You're really not all that *important* to them.'

I frowned at that. No one likes being told they're not important.

'Think about it,' Paddy insisted. 'The Cartel is a powerful magical organization. You're one teenager, aside from what else you are. They may be Enemy Number One in your life, but you're not that to them. They most likely see you as a bit of a nuisance, nothing more. A mosquito, to be swatted.'

'I'd like to be a wasp, at least,' I said.

He grinned. 'All right. Or a gadfly, stinging them now and then. But they have bigger plots and purposes beyond just hunting you.'

According to Paddy, the Cartel wasn't a huge organization. There'd be a fair number of underlings, he reckoned – minor mages with limited abilities, along with the demons and other servants – but with probably only about a dozen or so high-level sorcerers at the top.

But that ruling group would be hugely powerful, magically. And would gain even more power from working together than they would have had separately. Which they used to go after all the things that evil-doers usually want. Wealth, of course, and also other kinds of non-magical power.

'Think of the Cartel as a magical Mafia,' Paddy once told me. 'Then you'll understand what they are, what they want.'

He didn't think that the Cartel had dreams of ruling the world, like comic-book villains. But they did sometimes use their magic to control important events. And not so long ago we had a chilling reminder of exactly that.

I'd gone down to watch TV with Paddy and Julia, and found that the news was showing a press conference where some politician was raving about a 'success story'. A group of companies that made and sold arms, with big-money backing from the government, was about to earn billions selling new sorts of bombs and guns and warplanes and things to some foreign country. And Paddy was furious.

'Governments are supposed to do things that benefit the people!' he growled. 'But where's the good in this? Selling arms so that some other country can start a war, filling the pockets of a lot of rich—'

Then he stopped and sat up, pointing at the screen with a finger that shook slightly. 'Look, there, that one . . .' he said.

The politician had made way for a new speaker, a

youngish businessman with smooth fair hair and a salesman's smile. But Paddy was pointing at someone else, sitting beside the new speaker. A heavily built man in an elegant suit, with a shaved gleaming head and a glint of cruel amusement in his eyes.

'I saw that one, once,' Paddy muttered, 'coming out of a posh restaurant looking pleased with himself. And I could sense the evil in him, all around him, like an invisible cloud. And the *power*. He's a high-level sorcerer – and I'd bet my life that he's in the Cartel.'

'So they've got their hooks into the arms trade,' Julia whispered.

'Maybe into the government too,' Paddy growled.

But the news moved on to another topic, and they said nothing more, as if they'd decided not to get worked up about it. So I did the same. I never paid much attention to politics or business anyway. They might all be crooked evil-doers, for all I knew.

It was funny, though, when two days later the big arms sale totally collapsed. The politician who'd spoken on TV was found – by a reporter after a tip-off – in a sleazy nightclub with a woman who wasn't his wife. Also with the fair-haired businessman and an impor-tant official from the foreign country, all of them drunk and on drugs. The scandal made the foreign country turn its back on the whole deal.

But the other man, the one Paddy thought was in

the Cartel, wasn't involved in the scandal and more or less disappeared from view. And, strangely, so did the mystery woman. No one even discovered her name.

But the papers described her as very attractive, with colourful clothes, big green eyes and wild red-gold hair . . .

6

That victory almost made me feel some liking for Manta, for a moment. But all that had been back in the early autumn – and now, in dank October, I wasn't thinking about Manta's victories. I was hoping for one of my own, with the slithery new stalker on my trail.

At least I thought he was. But a few days after the chase over the fences, I went out to a street market where I sometimes got odd jobs to earn a bit of cash, and didn't have a sniff of danger all day long.

Next morning, feeling lazy, I wandered downstairs to see if I could watch one of Paddy's DVDs. He had a mass of them, lots of fantasy and horror and sci-fi. But Paddy wasn't there, and I knew I'd make Julia uneasy if I hung around. So, instead, I decided to visit the library.

My schooling was patchy till I was eleven and then non-existent, until I started trying to educate myself. Paddy helped with that too. So I'd got to like reading books, and it suited me. I could do it alone, anywhere, without needing machinery or even electricity in daylight. And library books are free.

As I often did when there was danger around, I carried the knife in my hand when I went out. But I wasn't worried. The library wasn't far away, I'd seen no sign of the new hunter the day before, and I didn't plan to be out long.

So I wasn't thinking about magical danger when I turned into a corner shop to get a bottle of water. I wasn't thinking about much at all. I'd been feeling cosy and safe for too long, at Paddy's, and I wasn't as alert as I should have been.

I didn't pay any attention to the thin kid wearing a long black coat, hunched by the door of the shop. I didn't notice that I was alone in the aisle where the bottles of water were. I only vaguely felt that the aisle didn't seem all that well lit, and that there was a cold draught . . .

But I did finally see the golden glow of the knife, reflected on the glass front of the fridge, and turned just in time.

The kid in the long coat was leaping at me, his oval eyes glowing like searchlights.

Because he was Cartel, he wasn't entirely human. He was hairless, with a mottled greenish tinge to his skin as if he was part-reptile. Though I was looking mostly at the rows of needle-teeth in his open mouth, and the shiny claws at his fingertips. I saw all that in a half-second glance. Then I threw a water bottle in his face and ran.

Clearly he was an expert tracker, so I wasn't likely to get away from him. But tackling a monster in daylight, in a shop with ordinary people around, was a poor idea. I needed a different battleground.

Being chased helped me pick up my pace, especially when reptile-boy looked more speedy lizard than plodding tortoise. Anyway, when I glanced back I didn't see him. Maybe he'd paused to wrap himself up before going past the people at the checkout. Though they might not have noticed him, since they'd all been staring after me. Probably thinking I was a shoplifter making off with something.

So I had a bit of a lead on him, and I used it to swerve down a side street – towards a multi-storey car park that would be just the place.

I knew the upper floors were unlikely to be full, so I hurtled down the ramp to a lower one. It was packed with cars and usefully gloomy. The dark, bare, stained concrete of the walls and ceiling seemed to soak up the feeble light from the few scattered bulbs.

Perfect – for an ambush. So, knife ready, I slid under a Range Rover and waited for him to come by.

The plan might have worked, against some other hunter.

Lizard-boy came straight down the ramp as if he could see my footprints. Maybe following my scent. But then he didn't start creeping around among the cars as I'd expected. He took the high road. Leaping from car roof to car roof in huge, high bounds, every one of them giving him an overview of a wide area of the floor.

I could hear his progress, and had a couple of glimpses of him from the shadows where I lay. But before I could work out what to do, the drum-sound of his feet on the cars went silent.

I couldn't see where he was, so I slid out again and crept along the row of cars. That brought me to the edge of the open lane that took cars to the exit, where I paused for a careful look around.

But he had leaped or climbed above the cars, up on to one of the ceiling supports. From that vantage point, he saw me.

And he sprang down at me like a panther leaping from a tree.

He landed that lightly too, flinging the long coat aside, eyes blazing and claws flexing as he grinned at me. And I saw, curving up above his head behind him, a long, whippy, muscular tail with a barb like a scorpion's.

7

That sight made me take a quick step back, slightly off balance. And he leaped, fast as a striking snake, his foot slamming brutally into my chest.

The kick sent me crashing into a car, gasping with the shock and pain. It felt as if a rib was broken, stabbing me inside. As I fought the pain, trying to gather myself, he kicked me again on the side of the knee. I felt that bone crack as well and cried out, sagging against the car, retching with the double agony.

His toothy grin widened. 'Can *you* be the killer that Manta made?' he said, his voice breathy and mocking. 'Hiding like a rabbit? Unable to fight?'

I gritted my teeth, panting. The pain was already starting to fade, but I stayed just as I was, waiting for my damaged leg to recover. And developing an idea . . .

'The Changeless Boy, they call you,' he went on, a sneer in his voice. 'But where others have failed, I will not. I am Chlar, and *I* will change you.'

His tail lifted higher, writhing like a snake, a smear of something dark on the barbed end of it.

'The point is poisoned,' he hissed. 'You will die slowly, in agony. And death changes everything, forever.'

I nearly smiled through my pain. The Cartel still didn't seem to have worked out the full meaning of 'changeless'. Or maybe they just didn't believe Manta's magic could do so much. And so, like some of their other hunters, this lizard-boy Chlar didn't get it.

A *fast*-acting poison might have killed me off before the magic that made me changeless did its restoring work. But a sadistic *slow*-acting one wouldn't.

And also, Chlar liked the sound of his own voice too much. His boasting was giving me time. I was still hurting, but I was mending.

'You lot think you're all super-killers.' I made my voice sound agonized, aiming to gain more recovery time and maybe also some information. 'But I'm still here. And none of you can even *find* Manta, let alone kill her.'

'The witch and her little magics,' he sneered, 'who dares not even spill blood. She will die before long.'

Then his eyes flared with suspicion at my getting suddenly conversational.

And I whirled and ran.

The fact that I wasn't crippled any more held him

motionless with shock for just long enough to give me a good start. I sprinted along the open lane and up the ramp, hearing his light footsteps racing after me. I suspected that he was gaining as I continued on upwards. But for all his agile speed I got to the topmost level still ahead of him.

The area was open, roofless, and I saw that the sky had grown heavy with dark October cloud. Also, as usual with a demon stalker around, extra shadows were gathering that had nothing to do with clouds, and it was colder.

I fled across the empty space towards what I was looking for – the low concrete wall at the edge. Still clutching the knife, as I had been all along, I leaped up on to the flat top of the wall, peering over.

There were no drainpipes or anything that would get me down to the ground, and the new brick of that wall was too smooth for me to climb. But I'd expected that. Just as I'd expected Chlar to follow me on to the wall – as he did, in another light-footed leap, once again grinning in savage triumph.

This time there was no talk. He clamped his clawed fingers painfully on my upper arms, the deadly tail curving high.

But I didn't try to fight his grip or even push him away.

I threw my arms around him.

Startled, he hesitated again, just long enough. I swept the knife down behind him in a furious slash, and docked his tail like a spaniel's.

He screeched, thin and shrill with pain, and I tightened my grip on him. Then I lunged forward. Over the edge.

He went on screeching, all the way down.

I woke up a few minutes later, alone among dustbins in a dark empty alley. The landing had knocked me out, but I'd made sure that Chlar hit first, with me on top. With my head tucked against his chest so my skull wouldn't be shattered.

Whatever broken bones and other damage I *had* suffered had been healed and restored while I was unconscious. While Chlar's corpse had withered and vanished, as with Harne and all the other dead hunters.

I got slowly to my feet, sheathing the knife, not hurting but weary. Also, my clothes, which weren't changeless, were ripped and soaked with my own blood and his. So I went to retrieve his long black coat, which hadn't vanished because he'd taken it off, and wrapped myself in it.

It was too showy for me, but it was what I needed to get home without being noticed. And, later, someone in the street market would give me a good price for

41

it. Which would buy me another jacket and jeans from a charity shop.

Then at last, I thought, I could go to the library. And wherever else I wanted, without worrying too much.

It usually took a while – months, sometimes – before the next demon stalker picked up my trail.

8

'So you found out that your Manta is still alive,' Paddy said. After I'd changed out of my ruined clothes, I'd gone down to tell him what had happened.

I nodded. Chlar had been useful for that bit of information, at least. 'And another hunter isn't,' I said.

Paddy frowned at me. 'Don't start getting cocky, lad. That's a sure way to get killed. Especially if they send something worse, next time.'

My shrug was more like a shiver. 'I know that. I know what I'm up against.'

'Good,' Paddy said. 'Let *them* be overconfident, not you. Gives you an edge.'

Maybe, I thought, as I went out to sell Chlar's coat. But I knew the Cartel would always have good reason to be confident. It wasn't much of an edge.

When I got back, with some new (to me) clothes and a bit of extra cash, Paddy and Julia were out somewhere. So I headed up to my room, taking with me the just-delivered local paper that had been left on the hall table.

43

I knew that it would mostly be reports of the week's burglaries, brawls and muggings, in among adverts for double glazing and estate agents. But it had fallen open to a page where a different advert caught my eye, because of its first word.

MAGE.

It was the name of a new shop, in an upmarket area not too far away, selling mystic pagan New Age stuff. Magic stuff.

Flopping on my mattress, I stared at the word, thinking about magic.

Ordinary people, the Powerless, would of course be astonished to know it really exists. But more – they'd be surprised by what it's really *like*. As I'd been.

For one thing, there are different sorts. The *mind* powers, like Paddy's ESP or moving things with the mind or glimpsing the future, are one sort of magic. Quite a few people have some of that. Then magic can be in *things*, like Paddy's amulet or Manta's disc where the mark on my throat came from.

And beyond all that there's the so-called *higher* magic, using words and gestures and patterns and much more, to work spells and make things happen. And that's the really scary stuff.

But the big surprise about magic is that it isn't always

scary and powerful and dangerous. It actually seems to have a few serious limitations.

For instance, even the Cartel's high-powered mages haven't seemed able to do much over any sort of distance. Instead of reaching out magically to snap my neck, the Cartel has had to send their demons to deal with me face to face.

And though most of the demons have all had special non-human abilities, they've also often shown themselves to be dim and careless and inept, very capable of making mistakes.

Which was probably the main reason why Manta and I were still alive.

I sighed, picking up the paper, re-reading the advert for the new shop, 'Mage'. I made a sort of hobby of wandering into such shops, for a sniff around. Even into the low-grade ones like the junk shop where I'd first spotted lizard-boy Chlar.

Because, I'd learned, people with *real* magic sometimes hung out in such places.

Some did so because they'd set up as gurus, 'spiritual advisers' or whatever. Some went to buy special stuff that they needed. And I think a lot of them just went to sneer at the Powerless customers, who visited such shops for fun and had no idea at all that it was real.

Anyway, I went to magic shops to watch the real

mages. Of course they kept to themselves, talking about their profession, exchanging tips, comparing notes. But I'd got good at lurking and listening, and they mostly didn't notice me. Not even when I followed some of them home.

And I didn't worry much about being spotted by the enemy, in those places. The mages I saw in the shops were mostly small-time, without much power. Beneath the interest of the Cartel.

But I was interested. Because I clung to the hope that one day I'd see a mage in a shop who wasn't feeble or dim or half mad, like most of them. A mage who seemed to know what he or she was doing. Like the one who made Paddy's amulet – whom, sadly, Paddy no longer knew how to contact.

Basically, I kept hoping to find a mage who knew something about the Changeless spell that Manta put on me. And how to take it off . . .

So thinking about the new shop led me to day-dreaming about being free of that curse – all the things I'd be able to do, places I'd go . . . And when I went to sleep that night the daydream faded into the other sort of dream – featuring Manta. With an uncanny reference to what I'd been daydreaming about.

And with a warning.

9

Of course, I'd worked out early on that those weren't real dreams, though they were weird and mysterious enough. Manta was using her magic to get into my head while I slept. And she seemed to do it to *tell* me things – to give me instructions, warnings, lectures . . .

For all her glamour and witchery she could sound a lot like a schoolteacher in those visits. Or maybe like a scolding mother.

She also seemed to know a lot about what was happening to me. And though I'm sure she couldn't actually read my every thought, she seemed very good at guessing what might be going through my mind.

This time she was standing on a moonlit hilltop rising from a shadowy emptiness like a desert or a moor. Her hair and her long dress swirled in an eerily moaning wind, and her eyes blazed more brightly than ever.

'You have won another battle, my Changeless Boy.' Her voice came clearly despite the wind. 'Let yourself be proud of that, and learn from it. Give up your foolish notion of removing the Mark of Changelessness. Even if you found a way to shed your gift, you would regret its loss. Stop your search, accept what you are. Be glad that you are no longer Powerless.'

She was moving closer, so that I was focused on her pale, elegant face. 'What I gave to you,' her voice intoned, 'has brought out your special qualities, your courage and endurance and resourcefulness, just as I hoped. My gift to you has made you not just a survivor but a *warrior*, Nick Walker. Never forget that without it you would have died in the beginning, at the hands of Harne.'

She was closer still, and I seemed to see only the luminous green eyes.

'You will need all your powers and qualities again, my boy,' she breathed, 'in the dire struggles that soon will come . . .'

I awoke in a fury. There wouldn't *be* any struggles, against Harne or anyone, I yelled at her silently, if you hadn't made me what I am!

But that was the big trouble with her dream-visits. The conversation was one-way. Manta could preach and scold and blather all she wanted – and I didn't have a chance to say a word back to her.

Which was really frustrating. I could think of a *lot* of words I'd have liked to say to her.

Anyway, I had no intention of giving up my search, as she'd demanded – even though I knew it was fairly hopeless. So I was still keen on looking at this new shop, Mage. It was a nice surprise when Paddy said he'd go along too, out of interest. Or for a laugh, probably, since it was getting close to the end of the month, which meant that the shop would be extra-busy.

All Hallows' Eve – Halloween – always stirs up the wannabe magic dabblers. Though they'd be better off, and probably safer, just doing trick-or-treat.

When we finally got there, pushing in among the crowd, Paddy was having a chuckle at the people buying crystals or dream-catchers or books about druids. But I was trying as usual to spot anyone among the crowd who looked a bit more purposeful and pro-fessional. And I was wearing a dark roll-neck covering the mark on my throat, and keeping the knife sheathed under my jacket, so none of those with real magic would spot me.

Sure enough, we noticed two of them straight away. An intense-looking young man smiling to himself over a display of 'real magic wands', and a sharp-nosed older woman who was buying some fairly unusual herbs. Paddy casually brushed past each of them in turn, since the touch let his ESP have a good sniff at them.

'Nothing much, either of them,' he muttered. 'Little bits of power, but no nastiness.'

As we went on drifting around the place, we saw a noticeboard in one corner. It had a lot of the usual leaflets and cards about psychic healing and spiritual leaders and mystic gatherings. Paddy trailed his fingers over all of them, his ESP getting glimpses of whoever put them there. And one card stopped him.

'This might be something,' he said. 'Never heard of this lot before – but there's power here that *does* feel nasty.'

The card was handwritten in flowing script, inviting anyone interested in 'ancient powers' to a gathering (on, of course, Halloween night) of a group calling itself the Conclave. Which is a word, borrowed from the early church, that mages like to use for gatherings where they try to combine their powers.

Maybe, I thought, not all that different from a Cartel . . .

But though Paddy had sensed that this Conclave was nasty, he felt it was most likely just an ambitious but semi-pro group. All the same, if there was magic power there, it was the kind of thing I liked to have a look at.

I even allowed myself a moment's fantasy that I'd find Manta there, one of the group, with herself and her powers well disguised.

It wasn't totally impossible, I thought. It'd be a clever

place to hide. Any kind of real magical group would be the last place the Cartel would be likely to look for her.

So – because of those faint possibilities, because I felt safe from being hunted for a while, and because I didn't have much else to do – I decided to go along on Halloween night and have a look at the Conclave. And Paddy decided to go with me, saying he was curious about what such a group might be up to.

It was quite clear that he also wanted to watch my back. That was fine, though he didn't usually show such concern when I went off somewhere on my own. And I agreed when he pointed out that if I had an adult with me we'd have a better chance of getting in.

Which we did, in the end. And found a lot of tricks, along with a real treat.

10

As I'd thought, from the address on the card, the gathering was in a private home in the same fairly posh area where the Mage shop was. Not all that far from Paddy's place, but a very long way in terms of expensive houses and well-kept streets.

We'd dressed up a little for the occasion, so they didn't just slam the door in our faces. But we still must have been a strange-looking pair, not the sort that usually came to that polished door. The tall sleek woman who greeted us, introducing herself as Mrs Weston, carried a lot of suspicion behind her practised smile.

So did the even taller but unsmiling Mr Weston, when she brought him in to look us over. And so did the really huge man with the bent nose who loomed behind him, scowling.

'I'm sorry,' Mr Weston said coldly. 'We welcome those who we feel will share our beliefs and purposes. But I strongly doubt whether that describes you two.'

'Why do you say that?' Paddy protested, with a scowl of his own. 'You know nothing about us—'

'On the contrary,' Mr Weston broke in. 'You should know that my wife possesses some psychic ability. It's clear that you feel hostility towards us, along with a dubious curiosity.'

'And the boy is carrying a *weapon*!' Mrs Weston snapped.

'So we are certainly unwilling to admit you,' Mr Weston said. 'Gerald will show you out.'

The big one, Gerald, flexed his muscles and put one meaty hand into a pocket where he obviously kept a weapon of his own. Scowling even more heavily, he shepherded us to the door, which closed behind us with a crash.

'Having fun on Halloween,' Paddy muttered, as I drew the knife part-way from its sheath. At least its silver glint showed that the house held no one from the Cartel.

'That man had a touch of real magic in him,' Paddy went on. 'He can probably manage minor spells, and not pleasant ones. I sensed a sick, hungry eagerness – as if they're planning some dark-magic ritual, demon-worship or something. We should be glad they didn't try to keep us. Those rituals used to involve a sacrifice.'

I twitched, peering at the house. 'You mean an animal sacrifice, don't you? Not human?'

'I don't know,' he growled. 'The hunger they're giving off acts like mental interference, so I can't pick up details clearly. Anyway, whatever they're planning, there's nothing we can do about it.'

I grimaced. The idea of any kind of sacrifice sickened me, and I'd really taken against the Westons. But also I had a strange, unsettling feeling that I shouldn't turn away and leave them to it.

It was like a powerful, commanding *hunch* that there was something worth finding in that house.

'I think I'm going back in,' I said. 'Look around a bit. See what's going on.'

Paddy looked startled. 'You mean just creep in, like a burglar?'

I shrugged. 'Why not? I've done burglary, when I had to. And there's no telling what I might find in there. If they're magical and evil they could have . . . I don't know, useful information or something . . .'

That wasn't a very good reason for taking the risk. But Paddy was nodding as if it made total sense, and showing no sign of wanting to leave. That made me wonder if he had a hunch too, which with his powers would be clearer than mine.

But he still fretted. 'That woman has ESP, Nick, she could spot you. And you don't know what they'd do if they catch you . . .'

'Then I won't let them,' I said.

Paddy sighed. 'Just don't get trapped. I had a feeling that when they get started they'll be below the ground floor. In the basement. Make sure you have a way out.'

'Always do,' I said. And I slipped away into the shadows.

11

I quickly found that big Gerald wasn't the only protection that the Westons had against unwanted visitors. Their expansive back garden was surrounded by a stone wall, not a garden fence. And though I climbed it easily, finding plenty of roughness for fingers and toes, my heart sank when I reached the top. It had jagged chunks of broken glass sticking up, fixed solidly in concrete, like a huge uneven sawblade.

But I couldn't cling there by my fingertips for long, and I refused to drop back down and just go away. So, teeth clenched, I pulled myself up on to the top as carefully as possible.

Even so, sharp points of glass stabbed into my hand and gashed my shin before I found a tiny space to perch. That meant I had to stay still, teeth gritted against the pain, waiting for the bleeding to stop and the cuts to fade. It wouldn't be smart to leave a trail of blood inside the house. If I could get inside.

While I waited, I drew the knife and, balancing unsteadily, used its hilt like a hammer to break off some of the ugly fangs of glass. That half cleared a space so that I could make a fast getaway, if I needed to, without shredding myself again.

When the pain and the wounds had mostly disappeared, I dropped quietly down into the garden, the knife ready, wondering if I'd meet another dog. But everything stayed quiet, so I started creeping towards the house.

The Westons clearly liked big flowering shrubs. I couldn't admire them in the darkness, but I was grateful for the cover.

Especially when two blazing white lights suddenly flashed on and spotlit the garden like a stage.

They were probably automatic, I thought, and reacting to movement. I ducked behind a large leafy ball of a bush and held my breath. But nothing happened. No doors or windows were flung open, no voices shouted, no one hurried out. I guessed that the people in the house were too busy with preparing their Halloween fun to notice a light at the back.

Since I'd gone still, the lights went out. And I went the rest of the way wriggling on my belly from bush to bush.

I was looking for a stack-pipe on the outside wall

leading from a bathroom, since where there's a bathroom there's often an open window letting in air. And in no time I found one – a bathroom window, locked in a partly open position.

Best of all, it was a basement window, so I didn't even have to climb. The knife, providing its silvery light, also easily prised open the simple lock. In a moment I was sliding noiselessly inside.

I found myself in an alcove with a toilet and shower stall. Beyond its doorway I found a silent, dimly lit space with a white carpet and a heavy table in the centre. Stairs led upwards at one end of the room, and there were curtains of rich crimson cloth on the far wall, perhaps covering another doorway. And the table was draped in the same cloth, with weird occult symbols on it.

So that was what Paddy had sensed. The table looked to me like some kind of altar, and that meant some kind of ritual, just as he'd thought.

And from the muffled voices and footsteps that I could vaguely hear in the rooms above, it seemed that it was going to be well attended.

But then louder footsteps thumped on the stairs, and I dodged back into the little shower-room, crouching in darkness by the window.

The voices told me that Mr Weston and the faithful Gerald were on their way downstairs. I braced myself to leap for the window in case Weston had some ESP, like his wife, and sensed me. Or in case he or Gerald needed the toilet.

'. . . probably no more people coming,' Weston was saying as they came into the room with the altar. 'So you can get the girl, Gerald.' He chuckled unpleasantly. 'I'll stir her up a bit before the others come down. It'll be more exciting if she's aware of what's happening to her.'

Gerald grunted obediently, and I watched through the crack of the door as he lumbered past and went through the hangings on the far wall.

Weston peered after him, looking eager. He seemed totally focused on what was going to happen, and despite the bit of higher magic that Paddy sensed in him he didn't seem to have any psychic power. Certainly he didn't seem to be aware of me.

A moment later Gerald reappeared, carrying the limp body of a young girl with long brown hair, wearing something white that might have been a nightgown.

As Gerald set her down on the altar – where she stirred faintly, though she seemed asleep or drugged – Weston smiled hungrily at her. Then he stooped and reached under the table's crimson covering where it hung to the floor.

And brought out a huge, curved, over-decorated knife that might have been made of bronze.

The knife didn't worry me. Despite its size and sharp point, it didn't look like it was made for fighting. Nor did Weston.

But what the knife was most likely going to be used for . . . That was worrying.

A drugged girl on an altar – a ceremonial knife . . . It was obvious. Too obvious, like something out of one of Paddy's old horror films. Except, of course, that for Mr and Mrs Weston and their friends it was going to be a reality.

They were going to sacrifice the girl.

12

I stared, appalled, as Weston tested the edge of the bronze knife. It was all a lot worse than I'd imagined. I hadn't really expected them to be up to anything more than a bit of chanting, dancing around naked, sipping strange potions, maybe cutting the throat of a chicken and making patterns with the blood.

But the Conclave, clearly more evil than that, wouldn't have a chicken on that altar. They'd have a drugged, totally helpless little girl. And their idea of Halloween fun was doing horrible things to her with a huge knife.

So I was going to have to find a way to help her. Which meant, first of all, trying to distract Weston and Gerald . . .

I peered around as much of the basement as I could see, hoping for some useful inspiration. But instead, even more usefully, I had a bit of luck.

Faintly, from upstairs, I heard the doorbell ring.

Weston looked up, frowning. 'A latecomer? You'd best go up, Gerald.'

The huge man trudged away to guard Mrs Weston while she checked out the new arrival. The girl stirred faintly again, her eyelids twitching, and Weston smiled and licked his lips, hefting the bronze knife in his hand as if feeling a little impatient.

And I came out of my hiding place in a rush.

Though I'd willingly killed off a fair number of Cartel demons by then, I'd never killed a human. Turning petty thief when I was hungry enough was one thing, but murder was something else. Still, I was ready to make an exception for the creepy Mr Weston, if I had to.

And when my foot carelessly scuffed the thick carpet, so that he whirled to face me, it looked like I might have to.

His eyes widened. Because he had his bit of magical power, he was able to see the knife in my hand. But he could also see that it was smaller than his knife, and that I was smaller than him.

Face darkening with fury, he lunged at me, swinging the bronze knife like a sword.

I managed to dodge the wild slashes, getting close enough to grab the meaty wrist of his left hand, which held his knife. But in the same moment, his other hand clutched *my* left wrist, my knife hand.

Gripping each other in that way, straining and struggling, we stumbled around the room like partners in some weird, clumsy dance. He was fitter and stronger than he looked, well able to keep the silvery knife away from him while forcing his own blade dangerously close to me. I was managing to keep him off balance, but that was about all.

Oddly, he didn't call out. He probably felt sure he could take me, being taller and heavier. And I could see that he *wanted* to. Along with the fury, he had that cruel hunger in his eyes again. As if he could hardly wait to find out what it would feel like to sink the bronze blade into my flesh.

So I let him.

As our deadly dance brought us close to the table, he gave a mighty heave that slammed me back against its edge. One table-leg gave way, the whole thing tilted, the sprawled girl slid off it along with the crimson cloth. And I let myself seem more damaged by the impact than I was and eased my grip on his wrist. Just enough.

It was a tricky bit of timing, but I managed it. Triumph blazed in his eyes as he jerked his knife hand free and struck.

And I drooped forward just enough, so that the blade took me high up in my right shoulder. It was agony as the edge bit into bone, but I was ready for it.

As usual, I blocked off the pain, put it aside so it wouldn't slow me down.

In fact I made the pain worse by twisting slightly, to hold the blade in the wound. And with all my strength I smashed my forehead into Weston's face.

I heard his nose break and felt it flatten. Stunned and bleeding, he reeled back, letting go of me and his knife-hilt. And I turned the silvery knife in my left hand and hit him just behind the ear with its hard metal butt.

He collapsed without a sound. I didn't think I'd killed him, but I didn't much care. Anyway, I had no time to find out.

With a thump of heavy feet, Gerald was coming back downstairs.

As he appeared and took in the scene, he stopped in open-mouthed shock as if he had walked into a wall. And I jerked the heavy bronze knife out of my shoulder and threw it at him.

I've never practised knife-throwing, which is a really difficult skill. Anyway, I only carried the one knife, and it was far too special ever to be thrown at anyone. But at the sight of the red-dripping bronze blade whirling at his face, Gerald tried frantically to dodge. Which made him miss his footing on the last step and tumble in a heap to the floor.

Before he could start to clamber to his feet, I sprang forward and kicked him in the side of the head.

He collapsed as his employer had. Just as a wild shriek of rage came from above, and quite a number of feet started rushing towards the stairs.

Mrs Weston's ESP had finally kicked in, to tell her what was happening in her basement.

13

The girl, still unconscious, was lying in a tangle of the crimson cloth. I scooped her up, cloth and all. She was small and light, not hard to carry as I ran for the bathroom window.

As I heaved us both over the windowsill she half opened her eyes – sort of hazel, wide-set, glazed – and stared at me.

'It's all right,' I whispered. 'I'm taking you home.'

I meant my home, first, until she could tell us where hers was. But she sighed, her eyes fluttering shut again as I raced for the garden wall.

Even with her slung over my shoulder – the knife-wound was starting to fade – I managed to scramble up the wall. I got some extra impetus from the blaze of the intruder lights and the sound of yelling and screeching from the house. The heavy cloth covered any leftover shards of glass from the place I'd cleared on top of the wall, and I zipped over it with no trouble.

A few moments later, with Paddy looking relieved

and astonished, we had fled around two turnings and hailed a passing cab.

The driver looked uneasily at my bloodstained jacket and the half-asleep girl wrapped in crimson cloth. But Paddy said, 'Halloween costumes,' and waved a fistful of money at him. And away we went.

When I gave Paddy a murmured account of the scene in the basement, his face went grim and furious. 'Magical sadists,' he growled. 'Altogether too many of them, these days. You did well, son.'

I looked down at the girl sleeping against my shoulder. 'I might not have been able to do anything,' I said, 'if the doorbell hadn't rung at just the right time . . .' Then I saw Paddy's wide, pleased-with-himself grin. 'Was that *you*?'

He tapped his forehead. 'I sensed that you were about to attack someone or do something else totally crazy. So I thought a diversion might help.'

'It definitely did,' I said.

He nodded, still grinning. 'With all these evil-magic groups and organizations, all the Conclaves and Cartels, it's about time the *good* guys started teaming up as well.'

That night another Manta dream came to me, or was sent. It was quite unusual to get another so soon. It was even more unusual that this time I saw only her head and shoulders, her amazing eyes like wild green flares in the midst of a fog that coiled around her.

'Darkness is everywhere, Nick Walker, and dire new menaces.' Her voice sounded urgent, almost frantic. 'As the enemy grows more determined to destroy you, those close to you also face danger. Be on guard, at every moment. And be careful of the *girl*, the storm-child. Protect yourself, my boy. Protect them all . . .'

The image faded and I woke with a gasp. But then I got angry again as I lay there thinking about it.

If Manta felt she had to send me these dream-messages, I thought, why did she have to be so vague and cryptic? 'Darkness is everywhere', 'stormchild' . . . What's the use of a warning, Manta, I snarled silently, when you give me no idea what it *means*?

But then, I thought, part of the warning had been fairly clear. And totally chilling.

She'd said that the Cartel wouldn't now just be aiming their killers at me. 'Those close to me' were in danger too.

Which – if I could take the warning seriously – meant Paddy and Julia. And, probably, the girl. I'd wondered for a moment, when the dream-message said 'be careful' of her, if it was telling me to be *wary* of her. But Manta's last words had been 'Protect them all', which surely meant her too.

Great, I thought. Now she wants me to be a protector. When what I really needed was someone to come along and protect *me*.

14

Wandering downstairs in the morning, I met the girl coming into the hall from the kitchen. When we'd got home the night before, she'd still been half asleep, wrapped in the red cloth, when Julia had taken her into another room. Now she looked more wide-awake than I felt. And she was wearing new jeans, pullover and shoes, so Paddy and Julia must have been out to the shops first thing.

Properly dressed, the girl looked older than I'd first thought. Small and slim, but definitely not a little child. Perhaps close to my age – the fourteen-year-old me. And quite pretty, with her big hazel eyes and long shiny chestnut-brown hair.

She also looked slightly weird, staring at me with her eyes wide and wild.

'You said you'd take me home,' she whispered.

I nodded, surprised that she'd been awake enough to hear me when I carried her out of that house. 'This is

70

home for me, just now,' I said. 'But we *will* take you home, when you're ready. When you tell us where it is.'

She shook her head. 'I don't know,' she murmured. 'I don't remember . . .'

That was another surprise. Maybe the drug she'd been given had affected her mind. 'You mean you've lost your memory?'

She nodded, misery in her eyes. 'Almost everything. It's been like that for a long time. Except I remember that . . . my name is April.'

'That's a start,' I said. 'I'm Nick. Nick Walker.'

'Yes,' she whispered. 'And more.'

'More what?' I said, thinking she was getting even creepier.

'You are *that*.' She pointed to the black symbol on my throat. 'The bearer of the Mark. The Changeless Boy . . .'

I was amazed and annoyed. I guessed that Paddy had told her about me, but I couldn't imagine why he'd told her so much. In that moment I heard Paddy clear his throat behind me, and started to turn to ask him.

But April wasn't done.

'The bearer of the bright blade,' she breathed. 'Silver in your hand . . . Golden in the throat of Harne . . .'

I whirled on Paddy, who took a wary step back. 'No, Nick,' he said quickly. 'I didn't tell her . . .'

And with that I completely lost it.

No one except Paddy could possibly have told April about the knife, or that I'd killed a beast named Harne on that long-ago night when I was changed. No one except some other thing from the Cartel.

Or Manta.

I leaped at April, grabbed her shoulder, shook her fiercely. She went white, her face crumpling in terror because of how my own face must have looked. But also because some crazy reflex had made me draw the knife.

'Who told you about that?' I yelled. 'Was it Manta?'

'Nick, no, wait . . . don't . . .' Paddy said behind me.

I barely heard him as I pushed April hard against the door and screamed into her face. 'Was it? *Was it?* Do you know where she is?'

'No!' she shrieked. 'No, NO!'

And with that scream something like a giant invisible fist punched me in the chest, hurling me back along the hall.

As I fell, a furious wind from nowhere blasted around me with an eerie howl. Paddy staggered backwards as the old mirror flew off the wall, narrowly missing him, to smash against the other wall. The rickety hall table leaped into the air and splintered against the ceiling, the carpet rippled and tore, doors slammed and furniture toppled in the next room. And behind April the locks on the front door rattled and snapped and the door burst open with a crash.

Wailing, crying, hair streaming in the wind, April hurtled through the doorway. And the door slammed shut again, its locks clanking solidly into place.

Julia rushed in, white and speechless with shock as Paddy gathered himself. By the time he got the door open, there was no sign of April. And by then my berserk rage had cooled and I was starting to feel a bit ashamed. Along with feeling totally unnerved by that explosion of magical violence.

Which was probably just what Manta's latest message had meant by calling her the 'stormchild'.

Once again, a question began to form itself vaguely in the back of my mind. Not about how Manta had known April was there, since her witch powers could have told her that – but about why she seemed so concerned for the girl. But as before I was focusing more intently on a different question.

'I still can't see how she could have known all that about me,' I muttered.

Paddy sighed, looking around at the ruin of his hall. 'Because April is a *psychic*, Nick – really powerful too, in many more ways than me. I found that out last night. She'll have picked up stuff about you from your own head.'

I cringed a little, feeling even worse about having scared her half to death.

'You couldn't know,' Paddy said. 'I don't think *she* knows. She's definitely got no control over it.' He shook his head glumly. 'Aside from her ESP, that's an impressive PK power, too. You know – psychokinesis, moving things with the mind. In her case *throwing* things, as wildly as a poltergeist. And it looks like she can't control that either.'

I knew about PK and the other mental powers that some magic people have. And I'd read about poltergeists – the invisible 'noisy ghosts' that make scary noises and move things around, often destructively.

A poltergeist often happens in a house where there's a troubled young girl. Many experts think that it's actually PK, from the girls themselves.

There was no question that April was troubled. She probably had trouble in her life even before the Westons got hold of her.

'She's lost her memory too,' I muttered.

'Almost all of it, I know,' Paddy said, nodding. 'Probably because of something terrible that happened to her when she was younger . . . It's amazing she hasn't completely fallen apart.'

'Maybe she just did,' I said. 'Because of me.'

'Because of lots of things,' Paddy said. 'Anyway, the important thing is that now she's wandering around out there, in a bad way and all alone. So we'd better go and rescue her again.'

15

But it wasn't that easy. We spent most of that day rushing around outside looking for her, with no luck. And that became the pattern of the next few days, always with the same result.

Julia mostly stayed at home, in case April returned. Paddy spent his time wandering the streets reaching out with his ESP, hoping to get a psychic hint of her trail. And I hit the streets in a different way – looking into shelters and squats, derelict buildings and overgrown waste ground, all the known or secret havens of the street kids.

I was no stranger to places like that, and I'd spent time in several of the ones in that area before I met Paddy. So, as I hoped, I ran into quite a few kids I vaguely knew and who knew me.

That meant that I could ask around about a lost girl without anyone thinking I was spying for the cops or social services or something. But even though they accepted me, I still made many of the kids edgy. I always had. Street kids grow finely tuned antennae. I looked like an ordinary fourteen-year-old, but they *knew*, somehow, that there was something weird about me.

Anyway, I asked around, and they answered my questions from behind masks of cool indifference, and none of them knew anything – or cared, much – about a girl like April.

Paddy's luck was no better. He even asked Julia to go and check with some of the girl gangs that would never talk to me, and still nothing. But we kept looking, because it was something we had to do.

And along the way I was keeping a careful lookout of a different kind, checking the knife's colour every few minutes. April was a new worry, but the Cartel was a permanent threat.

Especially after that dream-warning about darkness and dire menaces coming my way.

All of that wound up my edginess to a fairly high level. I started carrying the knife in my hand again, a lot of the time, to keep an eye on its colour and have it ready. And though the knife stayed silvery I was always extra-careful after sunset, which came earlier in those shortening November days.

On the fourth day after April fled, heavy clouds and a hint of drizzle made mid-afternoon seem like evening. So as usual I was being watchful as I hurried along a side road off the main shopping area. And when I heard a strange hissing rush behind me, I whirled and crouched, knife ready.

To see a tall lanky kid in a hooded jacket blinking at me.

'Walker,' he said, a bit uneasily.

I straightened, sheathing the knife that he couldn't see. 'Blades.'

He was older than me, tall because he was on rollerblades, as he'd been every time I ever saw him. Maybe he never took them off. He was an expert snatch-and-run thief, and the blades got him away faster than an Olympic sprinter.

'You still lookin' for that, uh, girl you been askin' about?'

I smiled a little at how he'd avoided the usual crude slang term for young females. 'Still am.'

'I seen her, maybe,' he said. 'Lookin' like how you said. In that big old museum in town, y'know?' He grinned. 'Good places to keep warm, museums.'

And good places for visitors with bulging handbags and pricey cameras, I thought, ripe for a snatch-and-run. But that was his business.

'I'll take a look,' I said. 'Thanks, Blades. I owe you.'

He nodded, lifted a hand, swirled smoothly away. And I took off, not quite as fast, to find Paddy.

But neither he nor Julia was at home. And I was in

no mood to sit still and wait. If it *was* April at the museum, she'd moved a good long way from Paddy's house. On foot, since she hadn't had any money.

I wanted to get there before she decided to move again.

The afternoon was even gloomier as I set out. And with the bus getting held up in traffic near the city centre, it was nearly closing time when I finally reached the museum. But though a guard gave me a fishy look, there were still a few people going in, and I went with them.

It was definitely warm inside. And huge, on two floors – a maze of big rooms still fairly full of visitors standing or wandering in clusters. With all the people, the display cases, the big bulky statues and other things, there were dozens of places in any one of the rooms for someone to stay unseen.

But I felt that if April was there she wouldn't be hanging around in the midst of those clusters, gawping at the exhibits. She'd be huddled somewhere out of the way, like a nervous rabbit in a forest full of wolves.

So I started moving at speed, searching the edges of the rooms where dark nooks and crevices might offer hideaways. I even risked looking in the women's toilets, in and out too fast for any of the users to react.

After some time, when I'd been through most of the

upper floor and was starting on the one below, a loud-speaker voice announced that the museum was closing. As everyone began moving herd-like towards the exits, I went with them, more quickly, planning to wait by the door and try to spot her as she left.

The foyer steadily filled up as the visitors crowded in, milling around, squeezing slowly out a few at a time through the main door. I went to stand at the side of the door, watching carefully.

Almost at once I saw her.

Whether through bad luck or her ESP or both, she also saw me. Whirling with a flurry of hair, she fled, her slender form weaving neatly through the slow-moving tide of people.

Only then did I remember that the museum had a back door.

I went after her, with some high-speed weaving of my own and a lot of pushing.

She was moving fast, but I kept getting glimpses of her hair that kept me on her trail, and I felt that I was gaining.

I was so focused on the chase, on moving fast and watching for her, that I stopped being careful about *me*. I hadn't looked at the knife once since I'd got to the museum.

A bad mistake. The sort that can mean you don't get a chance to make another.

16

Several rooms on, I was halted. I was sure that April had run in there, but neither of us would be running out through the arched opening on the far side. An over-eager security man had already pulled a barrier across it, a metal grille. Which meant that April had been stopped too. In that room.

It had probably been the same over-eager guard, I thought, that had already turned most of the lights off. Just small security night-lights glowed by the doors, filling the room with shadows.

Still concentrating on April, I didn't notice that it wasn't warm any more.

'April, I won't hurt you,' I called quietly. 'I'm sorry I scared you before.'

Not a sound.

I sighed, peering around. The big glass display cases in the room were full of hand tools and utensils from long-ago times. A lot of them were eaten with rust, but some were in fair shape. And in a corner stood a much bigger case with dummies dressed like olden-day farmers holding more old tools, spades and hoes and scythes and so on.

I was sure I'd seen a flicker of movement behind that case.

I moved towards it, trying to look unthreatening. 'I won't hurt you,' I repeated.

Then I jerked to a stop, hearing a quiet chuckle behind me.

When I spun around, I didn't need to check the knife-blade.

I also realized that it hadn't been a security man who'd closed off the far doorway. Another metal grille was sliding, as if by itself, across the doorway I'd come through.

No way out, I thought, no chance to run. Maybe no chance to survive.

I was looking at a tall, imposing figure in a high-necked tunic and dark trousers. His face and head were hairless, his skin was death-white and shiny as if he was made of fine china. But he didn't look breakable.

As I stared, he raised his long pale hands – and they changed shape, becoming curved shiny blades. Like the short-handled sickles that people use to cut grass or weeds. But probably a lot sharper.

As if that wasn't bad enough, the whole shape of him

flickered and blurred – and suddenly there were two of him, perfect twins.

And then there were four. And then six.

'So you are the Changeless Boy. How very young you are . . .'

The six spoke in unison, their voices soft and music-al, their smiles placid, a look in their eyes that was almost sorrowful.

I said nothing, just drew the knife – glowing a molten gold – and waited.

'You will not know me, of course,' the voices said. 'I am Conrad. I am the one they send when others fail.'

'When they get killed,' I muttered.

'Indeed,' the voices said. 'You have had your suc-cesses.'

'And now the Cartel's getting desperate?' I asked. Sometimes an enemy will get careless if you can annoy them enough.

'No, young one.' The smiles remained peaceful as the six drew apart, circling around me. 'Now they have sent Conrad. And *you* are desperate.'

As one, with blurring speed, they struck at me.

But I'd anticipated, and I was nearly as quick. I vaulted to the top of one of the display cases, the glass creaking under my feet, then leaped to another. I knew I had to get out of their circle and stay out. Not that I gave myself any kind of real chance. But as long as you can stay alive, you never know . . .

Then all hope vanished, as their six pairs of arms stretched out unbelievably long, their sickle-hands extending into shapes like hooked spears to slash at me.

I dodged and twisted away from three, blocked another with my knife – and the remaining two sliced across my right shoulder and my side. With blood pouring from the wounds, and the pain threatening to overpower me, I fought to stay upright, hacking wildly at the closest spearhead.

It jerked back, dangling as if damaged, bringing a cry of pain from the Conrads. And I stumbled away, half falling, dodging behind another glass case.

Again the monstrous hands changed – two into huge hammers that smashed that case into powder, the others into spinning circular saws and long vibrating blades.

One of the saws ripped my jacket and shirt and skin as I flung myself away, but I hardly felt it. The pain, the noise, the blood, all of it seemed to fade – as if I had moved into a cold hard place where every feeling was muffled and remote. An empty place where death was coming at last to claim me.

Reeling, fighting to keep my balance, I struck out grimly at my attackers. Some of the demon-weapons drew sharply back from the golden knife, but another saw bit into my leg. As I fell, one of the blades flashed down.

I felt a thin fiery line drawn across my throat.

The blade pulled back, dripping red, and I crumpled, down into a pool of my own blood. Wounds on me took minutes to heal. With a slit throat I only had seconds.

I looked blankly up at the sadly smiling faces of the Conrads, and waited to die.

And every display case in the room blasted apart as if hit by grenades.

The eruptions flung huge shards of glass in all directions. And with the glass all the contents of the cases, all the ancient saws and knives and axes and chisels and scythes, were hurled spinning like a cyclone of metal through the air.

I was flat on the floor, below that terrifying whirling storm. But the six Conrads were standing around me. And I stared with disbelief as I saw them pierced and slashed from every side, each of them sprouting a mass of glittering blades of glass or ancient blades of iron, driven deep into the strange pale flesh.

One had his head almost completely sliced off, another lost an arm, another's belly was carved open . . . No blood gushed from any of their wounds, only trails of something like greasy black smoke. But all six were toppling silently to the floor, where their bodies collapsed, dissolving into the smoke, fading to nothing.

Then I saw April.

As wild-eyed as ever but unhurt, she stood with her back pressed against the grille that covered the far doorway. She was staring around at the wreckage of the room, at the places where the dead Conrads had dwindled and vanished. Then she looked at me, and took a deep shuddering breath.

I felt the burning fatal gash in my throat grow icy. And with something like relief I slid away into a welcome pain-free darkness.

17

When my eyes opened, I wasn't sure whether I felt grateful or disappointed. But at least I wasn't hurting. I was cold, though, because I was outside – lying in darkness on damp grass under a tree.

With April sitting beside me, shivering.

'Why am I still alive?' I groaned.

She jumped and squeaked like a startled mouse. 'I don't *know*! I thought those monsters had killed you, your blood was *everywhere* . . . And then the whole place blew up, and *they* were killed instead and sort of *melted* . . . !' Her voice was rising to a thin panicky wail. 'Then somehow your bleeding stopped, and your wounds . . . How could they just *disappear*? How could any of that *happen*?'

'Long story,' I muttered. 'And there are better places to tell it.'

But part of the story was astounding me, as well. I'd been bleeding to death from a cut throat. And it could only be that April had stopped it. That she had *repaired* my fatal wound, just in time, somehow joining the slashed veins back together. With the same wild magical PK power that had blown the glass cases to bits.

If so, she didn't seem to know it. She didn't seem to realize she'd done any of it.

Think about that later, I told myself, and sat up slowly, looking around. We were in a little park or square with trees and bushes, benches and paths. And with a spiky metal fence around it – except where something had wrenched the heavy gate off its hinges.

'Did you bring me here?' I asked.

She nodded. 'But I'm not sure how!' She was still in thin-wailing mode. 'In the museum I could hear people shouting and running towards that room, after the cases exploded and everything. So I started dragging you away. I was so afraid, and sort of dazed . . . But somehow I got you outside and found this place . . .'

And along the way, I thought, you smashed through a metal grille and probably through some side door in the museum and then the gate in this fence. Maybe you even have the power to keep people from seeing us. And you didn't know you were doing it. You still don't.

The thought of it made my insides clench. All that power – and no control . . .

Carefully I reached out to her, letting my hand rest unthreateningly on hers. She flinched, but only a little, watching me.

'You saved my life in there,' I said. 'Thank you.'

Some of the tension drained out of her. 'If I did,' she said, her voice almost normal again, 'it's only fair. You saved mine, on Halloween.'

We both managed small shaky smiles as we got to our feet. Then a thought hit me, a bit late, and my hand flew to the sheath at my hip. Where, to my deep relief, the knife nestled safely.

'I brought that too,' April murmured. 'I thought you'd want it.'

'You have no idea,' I breathed. 'It's saved my life a few times too.'

I slid the knife part-way out, glad to see the blade glowing silver, reassuring me that no more demon stalkers were lurking nearby. Lucky for them, I thought, with April around.

And as we moved away I was wondering – what if she *stayed* around? And learned how to control that power?

What a weapon she'd be, when the next killer came . . .

We walked home, because April had no money and my bus ride to the museum hadn't left me enough for the fares for both of us. Anyway, my clothes were too chopped up and blood-drenched to be shown so publicly. Once again I'd have to find a bit of work to pay for another visit to the charity shops.

We didn't say much, either, on the way home. For one thing we were trying to stay out of sight as much as we could. Dark silent night-time streets can hold other sorts of predators, not magical but still dangerous.

But also April was probably struggling with the closed-off places in her mind, trying to prise out a memory or two that might tell her something about her past and her power. And as usual I was peering warily at every shadow around us, with a knot of anxiety twisting in my stomach.

I kept thinking about what Conrad had said – that he was the one who was sent when others failed. He was definitely a heavy-duty killer, the worst I'd ever faced. No question that he would have finished me off if April hadn't been there.

But that didn't mean that Conrad would be the *last* one the Cartel would send.

It just meant that the next one would be even worse.

And I felt frustrated, almost angry, at the thought that April might not be around, or might still not have discovered how to control her power, when that next one came. So again I'd be on my own against some magical monstrosity . . .

I stopped that thought as if clapping a hand over my mouth. And the knot in my stomach turned into an appalled self-loathing that almost made me throw up.

I hadn't been thinking for a second about the danger to April. For all I knew, the Cartel had got a magical sight of the defeat of Conrad and now knew all about her.

When their next killers came, they might be coming for her as well as me.

But even if they didn't know about her, I'd still brought her into my life, on to the cruel and deadly edge that I had to walk. And here I was hoping, *expecting*, that she would use her power to stop the next killers sent after me.

I was ready to put a frightened girl into unguessable danger to be a protection for me, and a weapon against them. I was ready to *use* her, to keep myself alive.

Which was exactly – *exactly* – what Manta had done to me.

Our silence went on, but April started giving me quick nervous glances. I suppose some of my ugly storm of feelings showed, or April's ESP got a hint of them. So she looked relieved when we finally got to the house. And she burst into tears with the release of tension when Julia met us at the door, tears in her eyes too, and flung her arms around us both, hugging us fiercely.

'You found her,' she gasped. 'I'm so glad . . .'

And nearly lost her again, I thought, as Julia pulled us into the lounge, barely noticing my ruined clothes.

'We saw it on the TV news,' she said, her voice trembling. 'A big explosion at the museum, a lot of damage. And Paddy had one of his psychic feelings –' she peered at me – 'that it had something to do with you.'

'Mostly with April,' I said, which made April look a little nervous.

'You can tell us all about it when Paddy gets back,' Julia said. 'He went out to look for you. But he'll know you're here now.' She smiled. 'When he's out he keeps a sort of . . . long-range watch over me.'

That made both April and me smile as well.

'Now you're probably starving,' she added. 'There's some chicken stew left – I'll get it while you two sit down and relax.' She sighed happily, her eyes bright. 'I'm *so* glad you're both here, safe and sound.'

I glanced at April, and the knot tightened even more in my stomach. Because I knew there could be no such thing as *safe*. Not for me and not for April either, if she stayed around me. Nor for Paddy and Julia, if the Cartel ever found a way past Paddy's protections and came here after me.

I remembered Manta's latest dream-message, the warning – about the threat to those who were close to me. Maybe, I thought, it was time to stop putting other people at risk to save my own neck.

'Protect them,' the dream had said. But I could think of only one way that I could hope to manage that.

Maybe it was time to go my own way again.

18

But that was easy to say, a lot harder to do. I'd been running and hiding for a long time, and it was going to take a lot of nerve and willpower for me to turn away from the only place of caring and safety I'd ever found.

Like strolling up and putting your head on the executioner's chopping block.

Luckily, over the next few days, no new threats appeared. And despite the bleak thoughts that never really stopped churning in my mind, those days had some good moments too, in ways that I hadn't expected.

It started that very night, when Paddy came home and was just as glad as Julia to see us. I gave him an outline of what had happened, and he seemed impressed, looking at April with respect.

'The police put out their official view,' he said with one of his gruff smiles. 'At first they thought it was terrorists . . .'

'Terror, anyway,' I muttered.

'But since there wasn't any trace of any kind of bomb,' he went on, 'or any bits of a suicide bomber, they decided that the destruction had been the work – get this – of *super-vandals*.'

Despite everything we all laughed at that, even April, and relaxed even more. Which was something that Paddy and Julia could always make happen.

Somehow that night they managed to sweep away the fear and gloom and tension that had kept company with April and me on our walk home. It felt like being wrapped in big soft quilts full of kindness and concern and warmth, maybe even love. And April especially sank into it with joy. She'd probably been aching for all those things for a long while.

Which made her even more ready and willing, in the days that followed, when Paddy started trying gently to unravel some of her mysteries.

He used his psychic ability, mostly, looking delicately into her mind. But even without that I think he would've made a good therapist. He was kind and caring, and April was perfectly fine with everything that he was doing.

Except none of it worked.

Day after day Paddy kept trying. He sat with her – in the small bare upstairs room next to mine that he'd given her – talking to her quietly, listening intently when she had something to say, probing gently with words or ESP to see what he might stir up.

And every day he drew a blank. Her memory of the past went on being deeply buried, her ability to control her powers stayed out of reach.

I didn't sit in on any of their sessions, but they both talked about them with Julia and me. And most days, afterwards, we tried to loosen things up by simply having some fun. Maybe it was a bit risky, leaving the house, but Paddy worried that April might start feeling like a prisoner. Anyway, we were all starting to feel cooped up.

So out we went, the four of us, whatever the weather – to window-shop in the nearest mall, to rent films for evening entertainment, to sample local varieties of take-away food, to look at the streets and the sights and the people. And April loved every minute of it.

But back home again, Paddy went on getting nowhere with her.

Still, the good news was that every time I checked – which was often, when we were out – the knife stayed silvery, and none of us saw or felt a hint of a demon.

And it was also good that April fitted in with us so well. Paddy and Julia liked her a lot – Julia seemed more relaxed, as if enjoying having another female around –

and she liked them. And April and I were getting more comfortable with each other.

In one of the quiet times I told her about myself, more than I'd ever told anyone except Paddy. And though she seemed startled and amazed, she didn't seem upset. I suppose seeing what she'd seen during and after the fight in the museum had pretty much prepared her.

So in a very short time we were friends. We'd never be anything more than that, I knew. She'd be growing up and getting older, and I wouldn't. And life might always be too weird for both of us to leave room for normal boy–girl stuff. But it didn't matter. It was good to have a friend. I even tried a bit of amateur therapy of my own, just conversational nudging, trying to unlock some bit of her memory. With no more luck than Paddy.

In fact Paddy was clearly getting frustrated, as everything he tried failed. There was a strange inner barrier in her mind, he said, like a solid wall. Nothing he'd done had any effect on it.

So at last he decided to try something new, a slightly drastic step. He decided to try forcing a door in that mental wall – by hypnotizing April.

But the idea troubled him. Hypnosis, he told us, especially by a true psychic, will reach straight into the unconscious mind. And if by accident he flipped the wrong switch in there, he might well ignite another of her destructive poltergeist outbursts. Blow up the house or something.

So he and Julia both worried about it, and talked about it, though not with April. They didn't want to upset her in advance.

And I didn't add much to the discussion. Because by then I'd started having new worries of my own.

Once, as the days had rolled on, I'd gone out in a rainy late afternoon to get something for Julia at the corner shop. And I'd definitely felt that I was being watched.

I saw nothing odd, and felt none of the dimness and chill that announces a magical danger coming close. As I went home in a high-speed circle, trying to lose the unseen watcher, the knife wasn't showing its golden warning. But the feeling had definitely been there.

And if it wasn't one of the Powerless watching me – a cop or whatever – I knew what I'd have to do.

If another stalker had come prowling around, it was time to go.

19

But still I didn't leave right away. I told myself that I wanted to get a glimpse of whatever it was, or at least a confirmation from the knife that it *was* another Cartel killer. But the truth was that I wanted to stay around to find out what would happen when Paddy hypnotized April.

It wasn't just curiosity. I liked the girl, I owed her my life, and I didn't think it'd be much fun having a total blank where your memory should be. So I was really hoping that Paddy could help her get sorted out. But there was something else, too, that kept me there.

Those hazy, half-formed questions that had once risen at the back of my mind were still stirring, nudging me. The questions about the strange *hunch* that had sent me back into the Westons' house, and about Manta's peculiar concern for April.

And I was beginning to think that I might have an answer. Really far-fetched and probably crazy – but not impossible . . .

All that made me wound up and anxious on the day Paddy started the hypnotizing. Julia and I went out to the back garden – a patch of scrubby earth with a half-dead tree – just in case April's PK power went off and smashed up the place. And we shivered there without saying much for most of the morning, while nothing happened.

But at least I didn't feel any eyes on me during that time. And the knife, which I checked every few minutes, stayed silvery.

Hunger drove the two of us inside at last, around midday, to warm up the previous night's pizza. But we just got in when we heard Paddy calling us. Sounding pleased, not troubled.

We ran upstairs, and found April sitting on her mattress, propped against the wall, looking a bit limp and wrung out. With Paddy standing by grinning like a proud father with a new baby.

'Are you all right?' I asked April.

'She's fine,' Paddy answered for her. 'And I think she'll be getting better and better from now on.'

April managed a small smile. 'It was all painless,' she murmured. 'But I'm really hungry.'

'We were going to have . . .' Julia began.

Then she stopped, her eyes going as wide as Paddy's grin.

Floating through the air towards us came the left-over pizza, nicely warmed, brought to us by April's PK.

'I got past one of the barriers in her mind,' Paddy explained as we ate. 'The blockage that's been preventing her from getting *control* over her psychic powers.' His face tightened. 'And I got the idea that that barrier wasn't there because of something in her past. I think it was *placed* there, magically, for some reason.'

'Who by?' I asked, scowling. 'The Westons? Why would they?'

Paddy shook his head. 'I'm not even sure the Westons have that level of power. Anyway, the answers to those questions probably lie in April's memories – but those are still locked away in her mind, buried deep. And I can't tell whether *that* blockage, on her memory, was also put on magically or caused by something that happened to her.' He peered at April. 'A few bits of her memory have come back, and more might seep out past the barrier, now and then. But getting it *all* back will take a slow healing process over some time.'

April's face twisted. 'It's so *hateful*, having my whole past out of reach! And I still don't even have much real control over my mental power . . .'

'It'll come,' Paddy said. 'You'll be able to blow up entire museums before long, if you like.'

That only raised half-smiles. 'Paddy said you've remembered some things . . .' Julia said.

April shrugged. 'Being alone and hungry on a street, not long ago. Then being in some kind of shelter. And those people, Mr and Mrs Weston, taking me out of there, at night . . .'

'I reckon they went looking for a victim and got an ESP hint of her powers,' Paddy said grimly. 'The sacrifice of a magical person would make a dark-magic ritual far stronger.'

Julia looked a bit sick at that. 'Nothing else?' she asked April. 'Nothing from earlier?'

April shook her head. 'Not really – just a few vague impressions. Like of being held, cuddled, in someone's arms, when I was very little.' Julia's face softened at the thought. 'And a sort of nightmare scene, with this ugly fat hairy woman who had long sharp claws. I think I was quite small then too – and I was screaming, because she was sucking my *blood* . . .'

'I hope that was just a memory of a bad dream,' Paddy murmured.

But I wasn't so sure. Of course if the monster-woman wasn't a dream, she might have been a peculiar sort of vampire. But it could be that she also belonged to a place where you'd find a lot of part-human monsters.

And where you'd find quite a few people with the power to put a magic blockage or barrier into a child's mind.

So could April have been a *prisoner of the Cartel* when she was younger?

20

My imagination fed me grisly notions of April being used by Cartel sorcerers in weird foul rituals. But then somehow managing to get away, maybe through a burst of her uncontrolled PK . . .

I turned away from those thoughts. There'd be no answers to such questions for some time, Paddy had said. But I knew one thing.

If there was a new demon stalker now prowling around me, the last thing I'd want would be for it to discover April – and report back to its masters.

Because if she *had* escaped from them, I didn't want them to discover her while hunting me.

I felt like slipping outside right then, to risk some prowling of my own. To see if I could get a glimpse of the watching presence to find out if it really was a hunter. But Paddy had gone into celebration mode for April's new *awakening*, as he called it. He dug out some chocolates and a bottle of cheap but nice wine, and put on some music. And April was glowing as if it was Christmas and her birthday put together.

It should have been a good time. But I was too wrapped up in my worries and fears. And the possibility that April might have been a prisoner of the Cartel was once again stirring those same questions about her – and making my crazy answer to them seem a bit less far-fetched . . .

All that left me dithering and fretting. To protect the others, and April especially, from the new hunter – if it was one – I should leave. But if what I was thinking, guessing, turned out to be true, I'd desperately want to stay.

Caught in that impossible choice, I didn't think I'd ever sleep that night. But I was glad that I did. Because Manta arrived again, in another dream-visit, startlingly soon after the previous one.

She brought me another dire but cryptic warning. But, far more importantly, she unknowingly made a little slip. Which seemed to tell me what I wanted to know.

There was no fog or darkness or weird echoes this time. Just Manta standing on bare damp ground, wearing a long blue dress that swirled in a wind like her wild hair. With her eyes flashing as bright as ever.

'The enemy has gone to greater lengths than I foresaw.' Her voice was a whisper, urgent and trembling. 'Those who have come for you before, my Changeless Boy, have been altered humans – half-monsters, yet of this world. But now their evil sorcery has brought one from Beyond, from another realm. A different menace from any you have faced, fearful and terrible. It is *winter*, bringing icy death to all it touches . . .'

As ever, her pale face drew closer. 'Flee while you can, Nick Walker. Lure it away from the others, then flee again. I cannot come to your aid, I dare not, but I wish . . .' I heard a hint of a sob in her voice. 'Protect yourself, my boy. They must not take another child of mine . . .'

She vanished then, with shocking suddenness, as if she realized she'd said too much. And I lay awake for the rest of the night, replaying her words over and over in my mind.

The warning was fairly clear, for one of her messages. Something new was on my trail – something not of this world, bringing icy death . . . But despite that scariness, I kept thinking more about her other words.

Another child of mine . . .

It was creepy. It simply hadn't ever occurred to me, even with her always calling me 'my boy' and so on, that she could think of me as somehow *hers*. Because, I suppose, she had made me what I was.

But that wasn't as important as the word 'another',

which she surely hadn't meant to say. It meant that *they*, the Cartel, had already taken a child of Manta's.

Which must have been what she'd meant, on that night when she'd changed me, when she spoke of the Cartel taking her 'most treasured possession'.

She had been searching for that treasure, as she'd said, ever since. And maybe, just recently, she'd found it. Because, maybe, it had somehow got out of the Cartel's clutches.

But with the Cartel always on her trail she couldn't swoop down on a broomstick or something and gather up her treasure. So . . .

She'd used me. Again.

It had to have been her magic that got me to go out on Halloween night to look at a group called the Conclave. And her magic that put a compelling hunch into my mind to send me back into the Westons' house.

To do the job of rescuing her treasure. Rescuing April.

21

Paddy stared at me as if he thought I'd lost my mind.

'Manta's *daughter*?' he said. '*April*? Come on!'

'No, listen,' I said. 'It makes sense . . .'

'It really doesn't,' Paddy said firmly. 'You're making a huge leap with almost nothing to go on.' He held up a hand to stop me interrupting. '*You're* not Manta's child, so maybe this *other* one, if it exists, isn't really hers either. But even if it is, and the Cartel stole it from her for some reason, the chances are that it's still wherever they took it. Or dead.'

'But April was a prisoner of the Cartel—' I began.

Paddy snorted. 'We don't know that. That bit of horror she remembered about a blood-sucking hag was most likely a fragment of a nightmare – not evidence of a link with the Cartel. It's the same with the blockage of her memory – there's nothing to say the Cartel did that. It could've been some other mage – it could have happened naturally.'

'I suppose . . .' I muttered.

He shook his head. 'I understand why you have this fixation about Manta, Nick. But don't get carried away with it. In that other dream of yours Manta seemed to know that April was with you. So if April was Manta's *daughter*, don't you think Manta would've been here by now to get her, no matter what the risk? Wouldn't she think *she* could protect her daughter better than you can?'

I sighed and shrugged. 'Yeah, maybe . . .'

'Anyway, the really important thing,' Paddy went on, 'is that warning she gave about a thing from *another realm*.' He scowled. 'There are said to be demon-realms outside this world, and the greatest mages are supposed to be able to reach them. But that would take a big complicated ritual – and a bigger one still to *bring* a demon here from such a realm and make it obey. The Cartel would be going to an enormous amount of trouble if they brought in a new killer that way.' He shook his head again. 'Let's hope that Manta has got it wrong.'

But I knew that she had been at least partly right. I knew that I'd been watched. Something – icy monster or whatever – was out there.

And that meant that I should stop fretting about

whether April was Manta's daughter, and try to find out what it was, watching me.

So when Paddy went back to his psychic labours, trying to prise open April's memory, I went out.

Which turned out to be a bad move.

At the time, it just seemed a nice normal day. The weather had shifted, briefly, to bright sunshine that was more like September than November. And when nothing much turned up, and I felt no strange eyes watching me, I relaxed a little.

Maybe, I thought, this winter-demon or whatever it was didn't like the sunshine.

Talk about overconfidence.

So, going out and heading back, I was ambling along the main streets rather than flitting through alleys, not really watching too closely for anyone or anything that might be following. There didn't seem to be much point, while the sun stayed bright and the knife stayed silvery.

Over the pasta that Julia made for supper that evening, April told us excitedly how her control over her PK was getting stronger. And Paddy didn't seem too troubled by the fact that he still hadn't made a scratch on the barrier that blocked her memory.

He also looked pleased when I reported that I'd felt no strange eyes on me in all my wanderings that day. Even Julia seemed happier, as close to being relaxed as

I'd ever seen her. So I unwound as well, and we had another nice evening.

But in the middle of the night I was again jolted awake.

Not by the aftermath of a dream but by a sudden biting chill, as if an icy breeze was finding a way into the room.

When I got up to see if I'd left the window open, I glanced out – and saw a vague shape in the back garden by the half-dead tree.

Something tall and pale and ghostly as if made of mist or smoke, standing silent and motionless.

When I whirled away to get the knife, then looked again, the misty thing had vanished. When I pulled the knife from its sheath, its blade was placidly silver.

But I knew the eerie shape had been there. And the coldness I'd felt seemed to freeze my insides.

The scariest thing wasn't that, as I'd feared, I did have a new demon stalker after me. Nor even that it was a terrifyingly different sort of monster from all the others.

What was most frightening was that it was *there*.

Neither of the last two hunters, neither Chlar nor Conrad, had ever found Paddy's house. Now this new one, having probably followed me that day, was menacing everyone in it.

Standing there, shivering, I heard Manta's voice from the dream again, telling me what I should do.

Moments later, with the first grey smear of dawn appearing over the city, I was gone.

22

I just ran, at first. As ever, I wasn't carrying much – the knife in one hand, a carrier bag with a few shirts and things in the other. Moving in the long-distance runner's style, a steady sort of lope with the upper body as relaxed as possible to save energy. Stopping once or twice for a few moments, feeling the effects of not much sleep and no breakfast, letting my body restore itself.

And the silver gleam of the knife in my hand lit my way and showed me that nothing evil was anywhere nearby.

But it had followed me before, and I had no doubt that it would be following me again.

So I intended to be as far away from April and the others as I could be, when it caught up.

As the bleak damp dawn grew a little brighter, I tried to get a little farther ahead by grabbing an illicit ride, hanging on the back of a dirty old truck that was doing its best to make the air less breathable. When it turned the wrong way I dropped off and went back to running. I was heading for a truckers' cafe that I knew, on the inner ring road around the city. There I planned to look for a ride out of the city, and I had a bit of cash that might buy me a bacon sandwich.

But I knew that food and rest wouldn't do anything for the ache that I was feeling deep inside.

I was feeling guilty about taking off without a word to anyone, as well as sad about having to leave at all. I knew I was going to miss what I'd had, briefly, in Paddy's house. The warm feeling of not being alone, of being with people who cared a bit about me . . . The good times and laughter, which I'd hardly ever known before in my life . . . The chance of getting to know April better – and maybe finding out for sure whose daughter she was . . .

But I told myself gloomily that I should have known better, that such things were not for me. The ache I was feeling only went to show that I had no business making friends, getting close to people. Ever. I'd always put them in danger – and I'd always have to leave them.

So I tried to put the memories aside, along with the ache, and concentrate on what I was doing. And I felt some grim satisfaction in having made a fairly good start.

Or so I thought, before I got to the cafe.

I came to the top of a low incline, stopped for

another breather and saw it a short way ahead. The lights of its parking area made it an island of brightness in the dull grey morning. It wouldn't have been open long, and there weren't many trucks around it. But more would come, I knew. And one of them was sure to have an easygoing driver.

Then I saw a smaller light reflecting off the damp pavement at my feet. I looked at the knife in my hand and saw the tell-tale blaze of gold.

Just as the cold ghostly shape flowed out of the shadows between two buildings and reached for me.

It didn't look even vaguely human. A large swirl of shapeless mistiness, with two dark holes near the top that might have been some kind of eyes. It was reaching out a bit of itself like a pale tentacle, trying to clutch my arm – and stretching the rest of itself wide as if to wrap around me like a sheet. Or a shroud.

As I flailed the carrier bag at it in panic, I could feel its deathly cold. If it did wrap around me, I knew I'd freeze to death in seconds.

But when I slashed wildly at it with the glowing knife, it flinched away as if in a panic of its own. At the same time a big SUV barrelled past with headlights glaring – and the misty horror flung itself suddenly away, rushing back into the darkness it had sprung from.

I flung myself in the other direction, sprinting towards the pool of bright light all around the cafe. And when I threw a fearful glance back over my shoulder, I saw no sign of it.

Doesn't like the light, I thought. I'd have to remember that.

And in my mind I made a little salute to Manta, wherever she was. She'd got it dead right. An icy horror recruited by the Cartel from some wintry demon-place . . .

My flesh crawled as I recalled the murderous, arctic cold of the misty being. It looked as if the loss of Conrad had made me a little more than just a gadfly to the Cartel. They'd gone to a lot of trouble to finish me.

But then I shook myself, gritting my teeth. I'd faced the ice-demon once, and I was still alive. I'd worry about the next time when it came.

In the cafe no one paid much attention to me, though when I bought my sandwich the woman behind the counter gave me a sympathetic look. Probably because my ice-cold attacker had left me shivering. But the steamy cafe warmed me up, though I only managed one bite of the sandwich before stowing it in a pocket. Being hunted by a freezing ghost ruins the appetite.

I wandered the tables, where about six truckers were stoking up on huge greasy breakfasts and strong tea. The first two weren't interested in a hitchhiker, but the third, a craggy man without many teeth, was willing to take me as far as he was going. To a small city in the west country where I'd been before.

He was driving a large van, not one of the giant trucks, but it seemed nicely roomy up front. Outside the cafe I kept a careful watch all around while he topped up the van's fuel, but I saw no ghostly shape. And the knife in my hand was silvery again.

Still, I stayed watchful as we headed out of the city, and I was glad that the driver seemed a man of few words. And he went even quieter when after a while he turned off the motorway on to a smaller main road. It wasn't as fast, he muttered, but it was a nicer drive.

So he enjoyed the scenery, and I enjoyed the fact that we were keeping up a good speed, getting me steadily farther ahead of the frightening new hunter.

I was less keen, though, on the non-stop country music he played, and his non-stop smoking. He'd also filled an old jerrycan with fuel, setting it just behind my seat, and every time he lit another cigarette I half expected the fumes to explode.

In the end the mixture of smoke and petrol fumes got too much for me, and I asked to open a window.

The damp country air was a relief – for about thirty seconds.

Then the knife lit up like golden fire, and the misty monstrosity poured through the open window.

It flung out an extension of itself as before, across my legs, which instantly went stiff and lifeless with the terrible cold of its touch. By then I'd flung myself away from the window, slamming against the driver. He was howling with shock and terror, trying to push me and the icy horror away. But I managed to keep my left arm clear of the monster, and struck out with the knife.

This time the golden glow didn't make the thing flinch at all. And the blade had no more effect on its mistiness than it had on the air.

Still I struggled, trying to break free of the icy grip, trying to brace myself and swing the knife again. The driver's panic was making the van swerve back and forth across the road, but the creature didn't seem troubled. It was stretching itself wide as it had before, pulling me towards it, trying to wrap around me.

And an edge of it touched the driver.

His scream rose into soprano shrillness, and he lost control. The van thundered off the road, hit a ditch, rolled and crumpled and slid and smashed into a big old tree with a sound like the end of the world.

23

In the echoing silence that followed I was only half conscious, dazed with shock and pain – and cold. I was lying on what had been the ceiling of the van, because it was now upside down at the foot of the tree. The driver's door had been torn off and he'd been flung out into a motionless sprawl beside the van.

But if I had any cuts or even broken bones, I couldn't tell. Part of my body was gripped by a fierce deadening cold, as if turned to ice, and the rest was simply numb. All I could feel was the searing agony of my frozen flesh.

The ghostly creature had clearly not been damaged or even slowed down by the crash. It wasn't finding it easy to wrap itself completely around me, where I was lying in a huddle. But my lower body was wholly enclosed in the lethal mistiness, and it was steadily moving up around the rest of me.

I still had the knife in my hand, but it hadn't helped before. And none of the shards of broken glass or other stuff flung around me by the crash was going to be any more useful. All I could do was yell and flail helplessly as I froze.

And then the relentless survivor part of me, still operating in the midst of that final panic, thought of something.

In the first attack, the golden light of the knife and the other lights had driven off the horror. Maybe because a thing from a dark and wintry demon-place wouldn't have much experience of bright light.

But the next time, in the van, it had just ignored the knife. As if it had learned that light didn't hurt it.

Maybe as if it had realized that despite the glow, light wasn't *hot*.

I thought I knew, then, what *would* hurt it. And what I needed lay not far away.

While the misty iciness went on gathering me in, I fought the growing numbness and strained every muscle that I could still move. With agonizing slowness I forced my free left hand to stretch out, holding the knife by the blade.

Using its hilt, I hooked the handle of the smelly jerrycan that had also come to rest near where I lay.

It took a huge effort to pull it towards me, and another to open it. And it seemed to take forever to stretch out again to get the driver's lighter, which was lying beyond the can.

But at last the contents of the jerrycan splashed out.

Weeping with pain and desperation, feeling the deathly cold spreading over my heart and lungs, I finally managed to flick the lighter into life.

As I threw my arm over my face to protect my eyes, the whole front of the van – and the misty horror, and me – went up in flames.

I vaguely heard the monster's shrill hissing shriek, vaguely felt its lethal grip on me loosen and fall away. Still hissing, it shrank into writhing coils among the flames, dying, fading and dispersing like smoke in a wind.

While all that happened I was fighting my way out of the van, my clothes and hair ablaze, adding my own cries as that agony took over from the torment of cold. Some frantic rolling over the damp turf put out my flames. For a moment I lay still, gasping and sobbing, retching with the burnt-meat stink of my own charred flesh.

But the survival bit of my mind was still in action, telling me to move away from the van before the flames reached the fuel tank. Somehow I dragged my burned body over the turf, dimly amazed to find that I was still gripping the knife. I even managed to drag the driver – unconscious but alive – along with me, just far enough for us both to be safe when the van exploded in a mighty *whoomp*.

As if that had automatically switched on nature's

sprinkler system, it began to rain, a chill, driving down-pour. Which I found welcome and soothing as I drifted away into unconsciousness.

But I woke suddenly with the sound of sirens in the distance. Some good citizen must have seen the smoke and called the authorities, and they were on their way.

I sat up, looking down at myself. By then I was com-pletely back to normal, so I didn't see any leftover crinkles of burned skin. But I could see a lot of skin, since the flames had mostly burned my clothes off. So I took some of the driver's.

He seemed to be coming around a little, moaning and twitching as I pulled off his fairly new leather jacket and his well-worn jeans and trainers. Everything was a bit big, but not too bad. I knew the driver would tell the police about the young hitchhiker who had robbed him and fled after the crash. But he'd also be telling them about an ice-cold misty ghost that had attacked him. So they might not take him too seriously – and anyway I'd be long gone.

Besides, I'd saved his life, sort of. He owed me some-thing.

In fact I got more than clothes. In one of his jacket pockets I found a rumpled wallet with a fair amount of cash, as well as credit cards and other papers. I couldn't use the cards and didn't want the other stuff, so I tossed the wallet down beside the inert driver. But I kept the cash.

Then, once again, I ran.

It was nicer than city pavement, running over the grassy field where the van had ended up. It was nicer still to know that for another while at least, nothing would be coming after me.

And when the next stalker was sent, other-worldly demon or whatever, I planned to be a *lot* harder to find.

When I'd left the city, my only thought – backed up by Manta's advice – had been to lure the new stalker away from my friends. Now my plan was to make it hard for the Cartel to find me again, by staying on the move, drifting from one town to another.

It was pretty much how it had been, for me, before I met Paddy. Never stopping in one place long enough to be known as someone who'd come to stay. Definitely never making friends or getting into fixed routines.

Of course I knew that no matter how I kept moving and tried to be invisible, a Cartel killer might still find me. But in the past I often went months or more between attacks. And sometimes when they came I'd managed to dodge and run and vanish, and get clean away from them.

So I'd be dodging and running again. And locking away any dreams and wishes for things to be different.

The key fact was that after letting myself get semi-settled with Paddy and Julia, I'd been attacked three times within a few weeks, by Chlar and Conrad and the ice-demon. And only luck – and April – had kept me alive.

So no more settling. I could hang on to my dream of finding a way to be rid of Manta's spell and be normal again, so I could leave the country. But otherwise all I could do was keep moving.

Because the only other option was to give up and die.

24

I stayed among fields and light woods for the rest of that day, avoiding roads and farmhouses and villages. So no living thing got a glimpse of me except birds, a wandering cat and plenty of curious cows. But when darkness finally arrived to keep me hidden, I prowled into the next village I came to.

I hadn't spent time in the countryside for a year or so, but it all seemed much the same. They still didn't lock their doors. When I slid noiselessly into a darkened kitchen, the knife's silver glow showed me what had been left lying on the counter – the end of a loaf of bread, a half-full bottle of some fizzy drink and an unopened packet of biscuits.

A while later I was tucked up under a leafy shrub in another patch of woods, fed and comfortable. The rain had stopped, the leather jacket was warm, and I was as safe as it was possible for me to be.

I even had the foolish idea, as I drifted into sleep, that it might last.

At first light I had a wash in a small brook, zipped the jacket up to hide the fact that I was shirtless under it and went to find a highway.

I felt that by then I was far enough away from the place where the van had burned that I could risk hitch-hiking again. I needed to get to a town, so I could use some of the driver's money to get myself some clothes. Then I'd move on.

But over my stolen feast the night before I'd changed my plan a little. I decided that I wasn't just going to drift around aimlessly.

I was going to make my way back to the big city.

I didn't plan on staying. But I felt I owed it to Paddy and Julia to let them know I was alive and tell them what had happened – and that the Cartel's ice-demon had found their house. I reckoned that it wouldn't have seen April, and I'd probably taken off too quickly for it to have time to report back to its masters. Anyway, it hadn't seemed all that big on communicating. But Paddy and the others needed to know about it, to make their own decisions about what to do.

And that meant I'd have to go back. I didn't know Paddy's phone number, and he told me once that it was unlisted, not in the phone book. But I didn't think a brief high-speed visit would hurt, once I'd tangled my trail as much as possible.

Besides, I wanted to see how April was doing.

The sun was shining, not very warm but bright, when I reached the small city where that first driver had been heading. I took it as a good omen.

By that time of year all the tourists who flock there, to look at the great cathedral and the more ancient parts of the city, had flocked off again. But the streets were still busy with local people enjoying the sun as they moved around. So as I skulked along the back streets I got a few looks of curiosity or distaste.

But after I'd been to the cheapest clothing shop in town and bought a shirt and a few other things, then cleaned myself up in a public toilet, no one looked at me at all. So I could stop skulking and behave almost like a citizen.

That meant getting something to eat and finding a sunlit bench in a little park to eat it, then going for a walk to get my bearings, see what was where in that place. I also went to admire the cathedral and the old buildings around it, wishing I could find a secret nook in there somewhere.

I've often wondered if the demon stalkers would be able to attack me inside a church. Most likely. Evil magic existed before Christianity, and evil monsters too. Vampires are only troubled by crosses in the stories.

As the afternoon wound on, some big west-country clouds rolled in and a spit of rain began. As if the sky had suddenly remembered it was November. But by then I'd found a good big cardboard box and had taken it back into the little park, along with a cheap burger for supper.

The park's gates had been locked at the first sign of twilight, but I slipped over the fence easily enough, hidden by some straggly trees. Then I made a nest under a bush and curled up, just like old times. Feeling warm enough, listening to the wind, I tried not to think lonely thoughts and finally slept.

And that night Manta's dream-image came again.

She was wearing another long elegant dress, and standing on what looked like a wind-blown rooftop. But this time the soundtrack wasn't working. She was moving her hands and muttering, as if doing some kind of spell, but I couldn't hear a thing.

More weirdly, and also for the first time, her dream-image wasn't looking at me. Those green eyes were staring past me, as if searching for something in the distance.

Then her dream-image did something else that had never happened before. She began to cry. Great glistening tears, running down her face. Tears that turned scarlet, like huge drops of fresh blood.

Until almost all of her face had turned blood-red, and in the midst of it her mouth opened in a silent scream.

*

The shock woke me so fast it almost flung me out of the cardboard box. And the gory image stayed clear in my mind as I huddled there, watching the grey light of a cool damp morning seep into the park.

Was this, I wondered, another cryptic message? Another warning? That thought didn't do much for my shivering. She'd been right about the wintry demon, so was some new horror after me? Something that liked spilling blood?

But that was nothing new, I thought. Every attack I'd ever faced had spilt a lot of blood. Mostly mine. I didn't see why Manta would send me one of her cryptic eerie messages about something that, for me, was all too familiar.

Anyway, this time she hadn't just been cryptic. She hadn't spoken at all, or even looked at me.

Then it dawned on me. Because this time had been so totally different from every other, maybe this one *wasn't* Manta with a message.

Maybe it was just a good old ordinary nightmare, out of my own head. So I told myself that it was nothing to worry about. And I tried to forget about it as I wandered back into the streets. A steamy little cafe provided a bit of toast for breakfast. Then, with the city awake and active, getting on with its new day, I went to the library.

I hadn't forgotten that the last time I'd set out to a

library I'd been intercepted by the lizard-killer Chlar. But I'd covered a lot of ground since then, and the knife-blade was entirely silver.

Besides, a library is one of the best places to spend a winter day in a strange town. As well as providing books to read it's usually warm, the other people there are quiet and there are places to sit. And as long as you don't steal the books or throw up on the carpet the librarians mostly leave you alone.

After visiting the library's toilet for a wash in hot water, I found a corner with a little table and a couple of chairs. Looking through a local paper that I took from a rack, I saw no report of a crash-and-robbery on a west-country highway. Too far beyond the paper's concerns, I thought.

So no one in that city would be looking out for someone like me. I'd be all right for a day or so . . .

A sound made me look up. A heavy-set middle-aged man with a shaved head had calmly sat down on the other chair at my table. His dark suit looked expensive, his whole manner looked confident and powerful.

'I hope you don't mind if I join you?' His voice was smooth and deep.

I said nothing, watching him blankly, gathering myself. Probably some kind of do-gooder, I thought, or a pervert.

Then his thick lips curved in a smile, with just a hint of cruel laughter in it . . .

And I recognized that smile. I'd seen it before, on TV, some while ago, when the news was showing a press conference about an arms deal worth billions.

I slid the knife part-way from its sheath, and saw that Paddy had been right in what he'd said about the man when we'd seen him on TV. The blade's edge was showing a tinge of gold.

The bald man glanced at it too, and I knew that he could see it. His smile took on a clearer edge of cruelty. As if he knew I was scared, and he was enjoying it.

'My name is Mr Redman,' he said, 'and I expect you know where I'm from.'

And as he spoke I realized what my nightmare about Manta might have meant.

Every bit of his visible skin – head, face, hands, neck – turned the gleaming bright scarlet colour of fresh blood.

25

Along with his gruesome skin colour, the whites of his eyes had turned entirely black and the pupils were slitted like a goat's. The teeth behind the nasty smile were also shiny-black, sharp as a shark's.

He could have killed me where I sat, since for an instant I froze with the shock of it. Instead, he raised a scarlet hand.

'I don't seek to harm you,' he murmured. 'Indeed, I couldn't even if I wished. Look closely. This is merely an image, a *projection*, sent to speak with you. That's why your knife has only partly changed colour. I cannot wield magical power in this form.'

I narrowed my eyes. The knife *was* only tinged with gold. And it did seem that his shape wasn't entirely solid. I could see a hint of the back of the chair where he sat, showing through his body.

That didn't make me any less frightened. But since he wasn't actually attacking me, I waited. Something was going on, and I wanted to know what it was.

'In any case,' Mr Redman went on, still smiling, 'you have shown an admirable facility for remaining *un*harmed, no matter who I send after you.'

That jolted me more than anything. '*You* send . . . ?' I repeated. 'You mean you . . . you're the head of the Cartel?'

His laugh was worse than the smile. 'Dear me, no. That's someone you would certainly *not* want to meet. No, I am what the business world might call a senior vice-president. With responsibility for certain special projects.'

'Like big arms deals?' I asked.

He raised a scarlet eyebrow. 'I'm glad that you follow current affairs. But most of my larger projects are rather more successful than that one. And along the way I attend to much smaller matters. Including you.'

'Trying to kill me,' I muttered.

Redman shrugged. 'That is so, yes,' he said. 'When we first learned of you, after Manta used you to kill poor Harne, it seemed sensible to be rid of you. When that proved difficult, it became an interesting challenge.' The black shark-smile twisted. 'Your latest victory, over the Skryl, was certainly unexpected. And, I might add, *enormously* inconvenient.'

'The what?' I asked.

'The Skryl,' he repeated. 'A bodiless creature from a frozen world. Not another planet in this universe, you

130

understand, but what you might call a non-human realm or dimension – which only very powerful magic can reach.' The smooth voice was sounding annoyed. 'You should feel flattered. It was a huge and costly effort to bring that Skryl to pursue you. And its failure is proving even more troublesome. Which is partly why I am here.'

I twitched then, because a nice-looking lady librarian was coming past the nearby shelves pushing a cart of books. But she just gave me a small half-smile and kept going, seeing nothing out of the ordinary.

I could feel my insides turning as cold as if I'd swallowed the Skryl. This was real power, on a high level, I thought, staring at the blood-red face. Maybe a higher level than anything I'd ever met before.

'What do you want with me, then,' I asked, trying to keep my voice level, 'if you're not here to kill me?'

'Actually,' Redman said, 'I've come to make you an offer.'

I stared at him silently, trying to work out what he was up to.

'It has been useful,' he said, 'to be shown the weaknesses of those employees of ours that you have . . . eliminated. But it would be wasteful to persist. Especially when I have come to realize what an *asset* you could be.'

I still said nothing, waiting.

'Quite simply,' he went on, 'we are willing to be useful to *you*, within reason – that is, to reward you – in return for a small contribution on your part.' He leaned forward. 'We want you to help us find Manta.'

I jumped as if I'd been stung. 'I've thought about finding Manta ever since she turned me into what I am. But I've never really *tried*. I'm a homeless fourteen-year-old, not a magical private eye.'

'You're quite a bit more than that,' Redman said. 'And, certainly, you *have* been in contact with her.'

I went silent again, because I thought I knew what he meant.

'You have dreams,' he said, confirming it. 'In which she speaks to you.'

That turned me even colder. 'You've been inside my mind?'

'Not as you think,' he said. 'But now and then, when we have known where you are, our psychics have sought to watch you, magically. And they have sensed the . . . *emanations* of Manta's magic, reaching out to you.' He chuckled nastily. 'I suspect she feels guilt over how she used you, and some responsibility for you. So she tries to help you, sending her warnings and messages.'

'But that wouldn't help me find her,' I muttered.

'On the contrary,' he said, still smiling. 'If you were willing to come to a place where our own magic can be more *focused*, where we can keep a constant – but not intrusive – watch over you, we would not only know when her witchery reached out to you. We could also track it back – to the place where that sending originated – and find her.'

I drew back, feeling even colder. 'Seems to me that if I went into some place of yours, I wouldn't come out alive.'

'Not at all,' he said quickly. 'We wouldn't harm you, I guarantee it. We would be *grateful*, because we very much want Manta, preferably alive. I mean no offence, but she is far more important to us than you are.'

'She's important to me too,' I said. 'If I ever found her, I'd try to make her undo what she did to me.'

'You don't need her for that,' he said. 'I'm not even sure she could do it. But I told you that if you help us, we will reward you. So if you really wish to be made Powerless again, that could probably be done. But it would be rather a waste.'

'A waste of what?' I muttered.

Redman's smile hadn't altered, but he was looking intent and eerily eager. 'Aside from the changelessness that the witch gave you, you have developed admirable attributes of your own. You would be a valuable addition to the Cartel.'

That nearly knocked me out of my chair. 'You want me to *join* you?'

'It would be the best thing for both of us,' he said.

'We would have Manta, and you would stop killing our employees. In return you would no longer be a lonely impoverished wanderer, endlessly in fear for your life. You would receive every benefit and luxury we can provide. Perhaps even certain *extra powers* . . .'

I frowned. 'Why is Manta so important to you? Has she got something you want?'

'Forgive me, but that is not your concern,' he said smoothly. 'I have presented our offer, and I do very much hope you will accept it.'

I thought about it. Benefits and luxuries, no longer being hunted, extra powers . . . Maybe even having the curse of changelessness lifted. It sounded really good.

I could almost hear Paddy's voice adding the next words. *Too good to be true.*

I was talking to a monstrous being who was high up in an organization devoted to cruelty and murder and dark evil power.

I didn't think that breaking a promise would be hard for them.

Anyway, I didn't *want* to help them get what they wanted. I may have felt hate and anger towards Manta for what she did to me. But that was nothing compared to how I hated the Cartel that had been trying to kill me for so long.

'I think,' I said at last, 'that if I was stupid enough to put myself into your power, you'd step on me like a bug as soon as you had what you wanted. So . . . forget it.'

His face went a darker scarlet, black fangs bared. 'That is a very foolish response, which you will certainly come to regret. When we *do* squash you like a bug.'

And he vanished, leaving me cold and trembling – until I gathered the strength to get to my feet and run.

26

A nd I kept running.

I used a bit more of my stolen cash to get on a coach heading south-east. Not directly to the city, but in that general direction. My plan hadn't changed even though Redman had found me. That seemed to make it even more important to tell Paddy what was happening, so he could work out what to do to protect the three of them.

So I sat on the coach and stared out of the grimy window without really seeing the farmland scenery, thinking troubled thoughts.

For some of the time I was grinding my teeth over what Redman had said about Manta. And I got bitterly angry at her all over again. Redman said she was probably trying to help me, but I doubted it. If she truly felt guilty and responsible, she could have come and put me back the way I was. So I could leave the country and be safe.

But no. In her dream-messages she'd kept on behaving as if she'd done me a big favour. And insisting that I should go on fighting the good fight, like her, against the forces of evil.

But she was fighting because she was a powerful witch who wanted vengeance. I was fighting, when I had to, just to stay alive.

And that thought, as the coach rumbled on, led me to thinking about something else, something more important, that Redman had said. Something that he may not have realized he'd said – maybe hadn't meant to say.

He'd been telling me how the Cartel became aware of Manta's dream-contacts with me when they were magically watching me. Which they could only do, he had said, '. . . when we have known where you are'.

And that seemed to mean that they *didn't always know*.

It was clear that they wanted to know. So whenever I managed to get out of their sight, away from their watchers, they'd have started using their magic to find me again. I grimaced as I thought about how often I'd made it easy for them, by getting stuck in one place for a while.

And I shivered, again, at the frightening thought that Redman had found me this time when I'd only been in one place over one night.

But, I reminded myself, he was a high-level sorcerer who could call on the help of psychics and who knew what else. Killer-monsters like the ones who'd hunted me before would need me to stay put for longer.

And even Redman and all the dark magic of the Cartel might have trouble finding me, I thought, if I just stayed on the move. No more stopping. Ever.

I grimaced at that bleak thought. It didn't offer much of a future. It almost made me wish that I'd never spent those few weeks in Paddy's house. I'd had a taste of something close to happiness – so it felt as if I'd been rich for a while and now I was poor again. Only now it was harder to take, because I remembered what it was like being rich.

But that's how it has to be, I told myself fiercely. Get over it. There was no time or room for self-pity. It's better than having no future at all.

Peering gloomily from that coach window, I remembered something that Paddy had once said. That no matter how awful the future may look, it only comes at you a day at a time. It was a good motto for a survivor – take life one day at a time.

One monster at a time.

But then I reminded myself that another good motto was 'Be on guard at all times'. Keep on the move at night, when hunter-monsters would be most actively on the prowl, searching. Get what sleep I could, as safely as I could, by day. Watch my back . . .

Putting that into practice, I glanced around at the other passengers. Not many of them, none seeming interested in me, though a red-cheeked grandmotherly woman sitting behind me gave me a little smile. She didn't look much like a Cartel killer in disguise, but to be sure I took out the knife.

Smooth and silvery, just as I hoped. I settled back, with the knife on my lap, to try for one of the daytime catnaps that would be the norm for me from then on. The warmth of the coach, the steady rumble of its wheels on the highway, began to lull me. Despite every-thing that had happened, my head started to droop . . . But I sat up with a snap when the knife in my hand suddenly showed a glint of gold.

I whipped around to put my back to the window, the blade poised. But there was nothing. Some of the pas-sengers glanced at me because of my sudden movement, but that was all. And the knife was only faintly golden, at its tip – and turning back to silver as I raised it in front of me.

But when I sagged back into my seat, lowering it, the faint golden glint returned.

And when I frowned down at it, puzzled, I saw why.

As I held the knife on my lap, the point of it rested close to the right sleeve of my jacket.

And on that sleeve I saw a tiny dot, perfectly circular, perfectly smooth and shiny. And bright scarlet, like a drop of newly spilt blood.

I jumped wildly at the sight of it, cold and sick with fright. I knew it wasn't my blood, or any other natural thing. It was too small and too perfect. And too exactly the colour of Redman's skin.

So he'd lied about his image having no power. Or maybe his actual self had been close enough to put it on me with PK or something. It didn't matter.

The fact was that they had put a magical mark on me that probably worked like a tracer, a *tracking* device.

This time, they knew exactly where I was.

27

I jumped again, even more wildly, when I felt a tap on my shoulder.

'You all right, sonny?' a voice asked.

I realized who it was just in time to stop myself whirling and lashing out with the knife. Turning carefully, I saw the grandmotherly lady, on her feet and looking at me over the back of the seat with a small frown.

'I'm fine,' I said. 'Thanks.'

'Only you been jumpin' around an' that,' she said, still frowning. 'Not on drugs, are you?'

'No,' I said. 'Just a bit . . . on edge.'

She nodded, not seeming convinced. 'Well, anyway – we're here.'

I looked out of the window and saw that the coach was rolling slowly into a dingy little station.

When I'd bought my ticket, 'anywhere else' seemed a good destination. So I'd got myself to a fairly big town on the south coast. It was often easy to find a place to sleep on a beach, even out of season.

I went through the town at speed, and quickly found what I was looking for – a sizeable charity shop. Where I amazed the lady behind the counter by asking to swap my nearly new leather jacket – 'too big for me,' I said – for a shabby, dated but serviceable duffel coat.

The coat had big pockets, which proved useful for pilfering a meat pie and a bar of chocolate while buying a small bottle of water. Saving money. As I took my feast away towards the seafront, I was fairly sure that the Cartel wouldn't realize that they'd lost me until they discovered that I'd dumped the jacket. For a while, I told myself, I was free of them.

And I was hoping to stay that way for some time, if I kept to my simple plan. To keep moving, especially at night, and to be watchful at all times.

But I still also planned to keep on, wherever possible, whenever it seemed safe, with my random search for help. Maybe it was foolish – but I didn't want to give up the hope, the possibility, that one day I'd stumble across a powerful but kindly mage who wasn't in the Cartel and who might know how to lift Manta's spell and make me normal again.

And pigs might get airborne, I thought sourly. But still – that thin hope had kept me going since the night of horror when I was changed. Now it could keep me going again.

On the seafront I drifted along the pebbly beach towards a headland that jutted out from the shore, some distance from any of the town's buildings. It offered the shelter of low tangled bushes, still with their prickly leaves even in November.

Pushing into the thickets, I found signs that others – dossers, boozers, kids – had also used that leafy privacy for their own reasons. But I was alone there, with food to eat, and the duffel coat was warm enough. Especially when I'd be sleeping in the warmer daytime. So I made myself comfortable.

I didn't do much more than doze for the next while, but it was enough. And I was on the move again well before dusk. After pocketing two apples from a greengrocer's I headed for the edge of town and soon got a ride in a farm truck. Still going more or less eastwards.

When the farmer dropped me off, at the turn-off to his house, it was fully dark. But I kept going, loping steadily along the highway, the knife in my hand to light my way and reassure me. If any Cartel eyes were checking on the tracker magic that had been put on me, they'd be watching a darkened shop where the leather jacket was hanging, in the town many miles behind me.

The thought made me smile as I ran. Even so, I stayed alert and watchful, every step of the way.

For all the good it did me.

I stopped for a few short rests as usual, letting my body restore itself, but still managed to keep up that steady lope for most of the night. Which brought me to a good-sized village around daybreak. A few early risers blinked at me with mild curiosity as I walked along the high street. But no one was looking as I kept going beyond the village, into a small stand of trees with plenty of undergrowth.

With birds making sunrise music around me, I found a shadowed nook under the trees that even offered soft moss as a mattress. Nestled there, I munched the second apple, knowing that after my night-long marathon I'd have no trouble sleeping.

But when I got to sleep, trouble arrived.

In the form of Manta, yet again.

28

Once again she was different from how she'd seemed in past dream-visits. She wasn't standing in some eerie landscape but on the ordinary meadow beyond the trees where I'd stopped. And she wasn't wearing one of her bright dresses, but a dark cloak with a hood covering her red-gold mane.

At least this time she was looking at me as usual, and not weeping blood. But, most strangely of all, her eyes looked more frightened than I'd ever seen them. And she was reaching out to me, hands trembling.

'Get up, boy!' Her voice had a spooky tone, but was clear enough – and urgent. 'You must get up! You must come with me, now, quickly!'

I got warily to my feet, wondering what kind of danger it was that was affecting her so much. She'd never seemed and sounded so frantic before.

'This way!' Manta said, her image floating away. 'There is danger near – and something you must see!'

I drew the knife, saw a faint hint of gold along its

edge, and glanced around. Cartel danger, clearly, but not close. And the Manta-image wasn't telling me to run. So was this another dream-warning of something coming for me?

Unnerved and watchful, I followed Manta's drifting image through the brush. And I was more unnerved when a twig slapped across my face and a briar scratched my hand.

Aside from Manta herself, everything was too normal, too *real*. Not weird and mixed-up and puzzling, as nightmares are. And the small pains from the twig and the briar clinched it for me.

The magical image of Manta was really there. I wasn't dreaming.

But Manta was rushing desperately on, half turning to beckon wildly, to hurry me up. I jogged after her, wishing she'd slow down so I could talk to her, question her. And though the golden glow on the knife's edge stayed very faint, I was getting more and more uneasy.

Within a minute or two we came out of the woods, on to an empty field with thick hedgerows around its edges. It was still daylight, but a sky full of heavy clouds made the day dismal and ominous. The field sloped sharply upwards, and I saw the tall shape of a building looming at the top of the slope, a dark silhouette.

Manta seemed to be heading for it, whatever it was,

so I followed, still tense and troubled. It turned out to be a rough stone tower, probably once part of a now-ruined old church, standing by an overgrown country lane.

The hazy floating image of Manta disappeared through the half-collapsed arch of the tower's doorway. And her voice echoed even more eerily from inside.

'Come! Quickly!'

Clenching my teeth, raising the knife, I followed her into the shadows.

I saw her image floating up a narrow stairway. The knife's glow showed that it was made of solid blocks of wood that all the centuries had petrified into a kind of stone. I was feeling a bit petrified myself, because it looked crumbly and unsafe but mostly because I didn't know what might be at the top.

But the stairs stayed intact and took me safely up. I found that the tower was roofless, open to the bleak sky and a chill wind that rose to whine around me. I hesitated, seeing that the floor's old boards looked mostly rotten.

On the far side of the open space, Manta's image hovered in a gap that might once have been an opening for a window.

'Come!' she cried again. 'Come and see!'

I moved carefully towards her, cringing at every creak beneath my feet. When I reached the opening, her image had drifted beyond it, out of the tower, hovering in mid-air, watching me, waiting.

I came to a stop on the broad stone ledge that would have been the windowsill. Fearfully wondering what I was going to find, I looked down.

I saw a huge roiling mass of dark vapour, as if the tower itself was producing a fog to rival the clouds. And I had the feeling that I was looking down into an enormous depth. As if I'd climbed far higher than I thought I had.

But still the knife only showed that faint glow on its edge. And I tended to expect a certain amount of weirdness when Manta was around. So I braced myself for more weirdness when she finally showed me what it was I'd been brought to see.

All she showed me, though, was a sudden smile – of a sort that I'd never seen on her before.

A smile of gleeful malice – and triumph.

The cold shocking realization of just how stupid I'd been hit me like a club made of ice. Just as the whole stone wall of the tower beneath my feet jerked and heaved.

The impossible heave flung me forward, off balance, towards the edge. I tried wildly to grab hold of something at the window opening, but the crumbling stone broke away in my hand.

And as Manta's smile widened, and the wall heaved again, I fell screaming into darkness.

I woke still in darkness, lying on what felt like cold stone. I wasn't hurting, so if I'd really fallen from that wall any injuries had already vanished. But that wasn't important.

Though I wasn't bound or chained in any way, I couldn't move. So I knew with bone-freezing sureness that I'd been gathered up magically as I fell, and now I was being held somewhere.

There wasn't much question who'd done the gathering, or what sort of somewhere it was.

I tried to struggle, but nothing moved, not even my eyelids. And as I lay there, trying to fight off the storm of panic that blasted through me, I heard a high, shrill, drawn-out scream.

For an instant I wondered if it was a late echo of my own scream as I fell. But I realized it was a girl's voice. And it wasn't an actual sound.

I'd heard the scream in my *mind*.

Then I tried to scream as well, tried again hopelessly to struggle, feeling as if my insides were being seared and frozen at the same time.

The scream had been a cry for help. And I knew that mental voice.

April.

29

I lay there for an hour or so that felt like days, while my panic-storm turned into a hurricane that threatened to blow my head apart. April's scream had stopped but I could still hear it in my memory. I had no idea where she might be – in the next room or miles away. But I knew beyond doubt that the Cartel had found her, that she was now, like me, their prisoner.

Which also surely meant that Paddy and Julia were dead, since I knew they would have tried to stop them taking her.

So much for staying alert, I thought miserably. They'd used Manta's image as bait, and I'd walked into the trap like a trusting idiot. And now this was it. The end. Like the sign that was supposed to be over the gates of hell, telling those who entered to 'Abandon All Hope . . .'

Whatever sort of Cartel lair I was in, I didn't imagine I'd be leaving.

Oddly, that final realization of my fate seemed to

switch off the storm of terror within me. And most other feelings along with it. Chilled, numb, emptied even of thought, I lay in the darkness and waited.

After another unguessable time, my stinging unblinking eyes felt a new pain, when a light came on.

It was a dim red light, but it was enough. It showed me that I was lying on a solid rectangular slab of smooth shiny dark stone, half a metre thick. The slab rested in the exact centre of the stone floor of a narrow high-ceilinged chamber with rounded corners, like a broad pit or a shaft. The walls were stone as well, as was the ceiling, barely visible in the red dimness.

Halfway up the wall in front of me I saw a narrow walkway with a railing, like a gallery, made of some dark wood. The unlit gape of an open door at one end of the gallery offered the only exit from the chamber. At the other end, wooden steps led down to the floor where I lay.

On the gallery, where the red light had come on, two groups of people stood staring down at me.

One group, the larger one, was mostly in shadow, not clearly visible. In front of them, directly under the light, four people were standing silently. Three men in dark expensive-looking suits and a skinny woman in a long dark dress.

I stared up blankly as one of the men stalked

151

forward to the railing. He was thin and stiffly straight with a long bony face, a lipless slit of a mouth and a mass of pure-white hair though he didn't seem that old. He also had the burning eyes of a fanatic or a psycho, glittering with the reflected blood-light as he gazed at me.

'You are now in the home of Mr Redman,' he announced. 'In a cellar, to be precise. A suitable place for one who has skulked like a rat through all his life.' He paused, like a performer, as sounds like muffled nasty laughter came from the others on that gallery.

'My name is Mr Fray,' he went on. 'My associates, here, are Ms Viney, Mr Blist and Mr Dyer.' He gestured to his companions – the skinny woman, a short grey-haired man, a tubby greasy man. 'You will recall that Mr Redman compared his high position to that of a senior vice-president. So we four, though all powerful mages, would perhaps be *junior* vice-presidents. With the emphasis on *vice*.'

Another pause for laughter. The thin one, Fray, grinned at me, showing small sharp teeth, and I felt my trapped flesh crawl.

'No doubt you thought you were clever,' he sneered, 'finding the tracking mark that Mr Redman put on you. But you should have thought that it might not be only on your clothing.'

He moved a finger, and my right arm rose by itself

into my view, the sleeves of my coat and shirt peeling back. I saw a small red dot, like the one that I'd found on my jacket, glinting on the skin of my arm. Vanishing as I stared at it.

As my arm dropped, Fray laughed, a high creepy titter. 'But you don't always *think*, do you, boy? In fact you're a blundering young fool. You thought it was truly Manta who came to lure you to the tower. And you thought that we hadn't found that grubby house where you were hiding, from which we have taken – *re*taken – the girl.'

That grinning confirmation of my fears for April fell on me like an avalanche.

And Fray saw the effect of his words, in my eyes, and tittered again. 'It's rather amazing,' he said, 'that you have managed to escape us, to survive, for all this time. But now your good fortune has come to an end. Do understand that aside from your unchanging body you are quite powerless. And weaponless.'

He pulled his suit jacket aside, and a lurch of sick anguish got past my numbness. I saw a jewelled sheath at his hip, and the familiar dark knife-hilt jutting from it.

'An interesting weapon, your knife,' Fray said, touching the hilt, 'which Mr Redman has kindly let me claim for myself. It will be amusing to discover whether it causes you more pain than other blades.' He readjusted his jacket, still grinning evilly. 'I hope that you now fully understand your plight. You cannot escape from this place, from the four of us. Nor, indeed, from our watchmen and servitors.'

Along the gallery, more red light appeared, illuminating the other group. It wasn't hard to tell which was which. The three watchmen were bulky men wearing helmets and armoured vests, carrying holstered handguns and knobbly clubs. The servitors were all in shapeless knee-length robes, not armed or armoured – and not entirely human.

In fact, one looked like the horrible fat hairy woman that April had told me about – with yellow eyes sunk in folds of flesh and long dirty nails like talons.

'You don't need to know their names,' Fray said. 'But you will certainly come to know their natures.' His face went stony-hard. 'Mr Redman offered you the chance to serve us willingly. Now, instead, you will be *forced* to do so.'

He nodded slightly, and the watchmen and some of the servitors filed out through the dark doorway. Then Fray twitched one hand, and at once the unseen power that held me down began to lift me instead. The stone slab vanished from beneath me. And I stayed like that, still lying flat, but hanging helplessly in mid-air above the stony floor.

Something like a spotlight, also crimson, blinked on

above me. My body jerked as my clothes were torn away and flung aside into the shadows. I heard an ugly titter from the mages on the gallery, and thought I saw a cruel glint in all their eyes. But I still couldn't move or speak or react in any way.

I could only lie there and watch in blank despair as the four sorcerers, followed by the remaining servitors, marched towards the steps that would bring them down to me . . .

'NI-I-ICK!'

The shriek, the sound of my name, made my heart leap in shock. I was hearing it in my mind, as before. In April's voice.

'Oh, Nick, I wish I knew where you are . . .' Her mental voice seemed distant, thin, hysterical. 'Or if you're even still alive . . . They've *caught* me, Nick, the Cartel . . . And I think they killed Paddy . . . I'm their *prisoner* again, and the same fat monster woman has been torturing me as she did before when I was little . . . Oh, please come and find me, come and save me again! Help me, *help me*!'

Uselessly I tried to struggle in the magical grip, tears in my eyes, groaning within myself, wishing I could scream aloud. If the fat monster woman was torturing her again, it meant that April wasn't just the Cartel's prisoner. She was *there*, in Redman's house.

But knowing that she was so close did nothing except add to my despair.

There's no help for you, April, I howled silently. No help for either of us . . .

I couldn't know if Fray didn't hear April's psychic cry, or heard it but didn't care. Either way, he was grinning again as he led the others across the floor towards me. With the light blood-red on his small sharp teeth, and glimmering in his hungry eyes.

30

The other three mages gathered around, watching, as Fray loomed over me, reaching down. Distantly I felt his clammy fingers trail over the hollow of my throat, over Manta's mark.

'Interesting,' he muttered. He brought the knife from its sheath – the blade was a blaze of gold, of course – and prodded at my throat with its point. I felt a thin trickle of blood.

'Obviously the mark is not just on the skin,' he murmured as if to himself. 'It would reach deeper, to the blood. So it could not be physically removed without ripping away the throat. Which would be rather drastic . . .'

I saw his eyebrows lift slightly, and knew that he was watching the small wound on my throat closing up, disappearing.

'And so you are as before,' he murmured. 'Unchanged.' He smiled. 'Yet you seem to believe, as Mr Redman learned, that your changelessness can be *reversed*. Which seems odd, since to achieve that would actually mean *changing* you.'

He turned to the others, still smiling his lipless, evil smile. 'It's a paradox, do you see? The Changeless Boy would have to be changed, in order to be no longer changeless!'

Even if I'd been able to move or speak, I would have just stared in silence. What he said left me even more dazed and shattered, because somehow I'd never thought of it. If he was right, there had never been a hope of me being normal again.

I couldn't be changed back, because I couldn't be changed at all.

But I wasn't able to gather my thoughts enough to consider things like paradoxes and whether magic could overcome logic. And it didn't seem to matter much. *All* my hopes had ended, in that place.

As the others dutifully chortled at his wit, Fray made a rasping sound that might have been a laugh. 'Did you wish to comment?' he said to me mockingly. 'Or scream or anything? Do feel free.'

Suddenly I could move – from the neck up. It was a relief to blink my eyes, to swallow, to lick my lips. But I was still trapped and helpless, looking up at a mur- derously evil sorcerer with the glowing knife in his hand.

'What . . . ?' I croaked, gasped, tried again. 'What do you want with me?'

His eyebrows lifted again. 'Well done!' he said. 'When you regain your speech you neither wail nor weep nor plead for mercy – you merely enquire about your fate! But then we knew you to be courageous . . .'

I said nothing to that, waiting.

'What do we *want*, you ask,' he went on. 'Indeed. First, I would say, we want you *here*, in captivity – so you will stop annoying us and causing us a great deal of trouble and alarm, as you have certainly done by killing our Skryl. We also want to *punish* you for causing that trouble. And we're keen to investigate the witchery that made you changeless. But, above all, having you in our power will finally enable us to find a way to your benefactor, Manta.'

I blinked, which was as much of a surprised reaction as I could manage. Most of what he'd said was obvious and expected. But Fray had also said that the Cartel had to 'investigate' Manta's magic, the spell she had put on me. As if it was something they didn't know much about.

The limitations again, I thought. They're not all-knowing and all-powerful. They might even make mistakes . . .

But I didn't want to start clutching at false hopes. At that moment I was focused more on how Fray seemed

159

willing to talk, to answer questions. It never hurts to know more about your enemies.

'Why do you want to find Manta so badly?' I asked.

Fray's face set like stone. 'Because she is *dangerous*,' he hissed. 'She is the most powerful witch this land has known for generations. But more – her power has developed in wild, unorthodox, *unpredictable* ways. And she is persistently using it against the Cartel, to thwart and damage us.'

'Good for her,' I muttered.

'You may say so,' Fray snarled, glaring. 'But the connection she has made with *you*, the concern that she apparently feels for you, will be her downfall. Your pain, your helplessness, will surely bring her to reach out to you. When she does, we will locate her.'

'Or maybe not,' I muttered.

'The magic is in place,' he snapped. 'It will not fail.' He smiled evilly again. 'We have already found you useful, by good fortune, in enabling us to discover and recapture the girl who was with you. We have searched for her for years.' His laugh scraped at my nerves. 'A probe of her mind will enable us to find and punish the foolish psychic who took you both into his home. But of course she is most valuable for her quite amazing range of powers – which will serve the Cartel, when we have made her one of us.'

It took all my willpower to keep my jaw from dropping. Fray was so busy telling me what they would do and how their plans couldn't fail that he hadn't realized what else he'd told me.

He'd let me know that April had been wrong, in her mental cry to me. Paddy hadn't been killed when they took her. And though the Cartel wanted to 'punish' him, I knew that with his super-amulet he was pretty good at surviving.

But also Fray had revealed that April was important to them because of her powers. So they weren't planning to kill her. They wouldn't even want to hurt her too much, in case that damaged her mind.

A small flicker of something like hope came back to life, deep within me.

With April nearby, and with Paddy alive somewhere and perhaps working out some way to help us, maybe there was some tiny edge of a chance, after all.

But then Fray was stepping back, frowning, as if vaguely aware that he might have said too much. 'Enough of this,' he snapped, and gestured.

And I discovered that I was going to need all the hope I could find.

The air around me was suddenly filled with ugly, sharp blades of many shapes and different sizes.

All spinning, vibrating, clashing, glittering, as they came down upon me.

161

31

The intention seemed viciously clear. I was being held in that place, stripped and helpless, to be tortured.

They were doing it partly to study the magic that made my injuries disappear. And partly in the hope that Manta, wherever she was, would pick up on my agony and reach out to me magically, so they could find her.

But definitely, also, just because they liked causing pain.

Fray was clearly in charge, and enjoying himself, as the blades set to work. And his magical power was huge, and skilled. There must have been over a hundred blades whirling around me, so perfectly controlled that none of them even brushed against another as they stabbed and chopped and sliced.

I was vaguely aware of more ugly tittering from the others, and of Fray stepping smartly back to avoid sprays of blood. But mostly I was just screaming at the top of my voice – with the monstrous pain of it, but also with a dim, wispy hope that April might be close enough to hear me.

But if she was, she wasn't listening. Because, as the blades cut and gouged at me, I heard *her* scream as well. Another distant mental cry, high-pitched and terrified, unheard by Fray or the others.

Still, I was in no condition to agonize over what might be happening to her just then. My own screams were reaching new levels, because Fray had made his blades vanish and had stepped back to let the others have a turn. And I found that there were worse torments than blades.

The tubby Dyer, shiny-faced and perfumed, seemed to like playing with fire, literally. He brought a lot of different flames to burn my agonized flesh, along with jolts of electricity and vile acids that seared and scalded. He especially enjoyed using a polished fingernail to pop the huge blisters that rose on my skin – and looked put out when my blackened ruined flesh began to restore itself.

Grey, quiet Mr Blist specialized in bones, and broke a great many of mine from toes to collarbone. He seemed a quite scientific sadist, measuring the thickness of each bone first, then timing their recovery. And just as Dyer had carefully made sure that none of his flames would kill me, so Blist avoided vital bones like my spine and my skull.

Skinny Ms Viney had a pinched mouth, a long nose and an avid look in her eyes as she stared at my nakedness. She was a poisoner, pouring grisly fluids into my mouth and nose and ears, dripping foul oils and smearing lurid ointments on to any patches of my skin the others weren't using, injecting me with syringefuls of agonizing substances. She also took care to do nothing so drastic that it would finish me off, but I felt that she often came close.

Through it all Fray stood watching, smiling his evil smile, making suggestions.

And the servitors hovered around being helpful, handing things to the sorcerers and wiping away spurts of my blood that smeared their labours.

The pain was endless, beyond description, and totally unbearable a lot of the time, so that I passed out quite often until they crossly woke me up again. Once I came around to see one of the servitors – short and scaly and wide-mouthed as if he was part-fish – dipping a finger in a puddle of my blood and licking it. Grinning when he saw my eyes open. Which made me close them again.

I have no clear idea how long it all went on. I lost track of time along with most other things beyond the endless agony and screaming. Once I thought I heard April cry out again, in my mind, and for a cruel blank second I couldn't remember who she was. Some of the time I forgot who I was.

But I suppose they weren't used to so much exercise, and in the end they got tired. So, eventually, when I awoke from yet another time of blissful unconsciousness, I found myself alone, lying on the cold stone slab again, in darkness.

I didn't need light, red or otherwise, to know that all the anguished flesh and bone of my changeless body had, as ever, got back to normal. Not the smallest twinge of pain remained. But even so I was covered in dried, crusty, leftover blood, and other foulness after some of the impossible agonies had made me lose control of bladder and bowels.

So as I lay there, still held firm by the magical grip, naked, filthy, shivering with cold in that stony cellar, the suffering hadn't entirely stopped.

From the depths of that misery a tiny flame of fury came to life, and I started crazily and silently yelling – at Manta. Screaming her name, in my mind. Hoping that she *would* contact me in another dream-visit, so that the Cartel could locate her as they planned. Then maybe they'd leave me alone. Or finish me off. Either way, the torture would stop.

But no green-eyed visions appeared, as time dragged on. Probably Manta couldn't hear me. Or maybe she was clever enough to know what they were planning, and was staying well clear of me.

Although, I thought, if April is her daughter, she might risk everything to try to save *her* . . . But only if she could find her. I remembered Manta saying that her 'treasure' was lost to her, as if magically hidden. If April was that treasure, they'd be keeping her well hidden again.

So with the realization that I'd get no help from Manta, my rage faded and the misery returned. Growing deeper as I thought about April and her torment. I even tried calling *her* name a few times, in my mind. I wasn't a psychic, so I couldn't send out a mental message. I was just hoping that she might pick it up.

But nothing happened.

Still, I was fairly sure she'd still be alive. From what Fray had said, she was important to the Cartel. And then a new thought struck me.

Clearly, when the Cartel first kidnapped her, she must have *escaped* somehow.

Some horror might have set off a wild outburst of her PK – as on that morning when she'd wrecked Paddy's front hall – and she'd got away. Now, having caught her again, the Cartel would surely have *replaced* the blockage in her mind, the barrier that Paddy had removed, that had stopped her using and controlling her powers.

They'd know, if that was how she'd escaped, that the first blockage they'd put in hadn't been perfect. Her power could break through it when she was terrified – just as it had in the two wild outbreaks of it that I'd seen. But in their overconfident way they probably felt sure that the new blockage would hold.

Except – her mental voice must have found a crack or something in it, because she'd called to me.

So there was a chance that she might break through again, despite everything, and blast a way out for herself as she must have done the first time.

I found myself smiling slightly at the thought of her freeing herself again, another setback for the Cartel. But the smile faded when I reminded myself that in her mental call to me she'd said she didn't know where I was, or even if I was alive.

So if she did manage to get away, she wouldn't be taking me with her.

And that thought finally left me just lying there, staring into the dark, mind and spirit empty of everything except the certainty that I was helpless and hopeless.

I knew I'd lie there like that all night, probably wide awake, unable to move. I knew that I'd suffer hunger pangs and desperate thirst. I also knew that I wouldn't die of hunger or thirst or lack of sleep. Such things didn't act swiftly enough to cause permanent or fatal damage to my changeless body.

I found myself wishing that they could.

Because I knew that before long Fray and company would come again.

32

But it was sooner than I expected when one of the dim red lights went on above me. And it wasn't any of the sorcerers coming down the stairs from the gallery.

It was the servitor I'd recognized, the fat hairy woman with the talons. April's nightmare. Probably coming to be my nightmare too.

She waddled over to my slab, staring down at me hungrily.

'You better now, right?' Her voice was harsh and thick. 'Hurts all gone?'

I said nothing, watching her. I didn't think she was asking out of sympathy.

'Yeah, you better.' She sniggered. 'You magic, hurts go away. Magic boy, special blood. Lovely blood for Elg.'

She looked around carefully, as if to be sure she was unwatched. Then she slapped a hand over my mouth to keep me quiet and used a claw to cut a gash in a vein on the inside of my elbow.

As the blood flowed, she clamped her mouth on the wound and sucked greedily.

In a few moments the wound began to close, healing, but Elg seemed to have had enough. Straightening, removing her hand, she gave me a blood-smeared grin.

And though I was limp and weak and sickened, I found the strength to ask a question.

'Do you hurt the girl like that?' I croaked.

I was ready to tell her a lie about overhearing Fray talking about a captive girl. But it didn't even occur to Elg to wonder how I knew about April.

'Some,' she said, snickering. 'She tastier now than when she here before, when she little. She much magic. Blood sweet.'

Then her smile faded, turning to a suspicious glower. 'You not tell Mr Fray. You tell, Elg hurt you bad.'

I doubted that Elg would be able to hurt me any more than the sorcerers had. Nor did I much care. I was thinking more about *why* she'd threatened me.

'Aren't you allowed to take her blood?' I asked carefully.

'Not supposed to,' Elg grunted. 'Mr Fray tell me *pretend* to hurt. Scare her. Helps him do things to her head, make her thoughts wrong. Make her his slave.'

That notion curdled my insides. But at the same time the fact that Fray wanted to weaken April through *terror*, not pain – and the fact that the bloodsucking Elg had access to April – had started to stir up an idea.

I made my voice indifferent. 'If they want to scare her they should've brought her to watch what they do to *me*. That'd do her head in, all the blood and screaming.'

Elg stared at me for a moment, looking startled, a wide horrible smile spreading across her face. Then she whirled and scuttled away towards the stairs.

Please let her go and tell Fray, I whispered to any divinity that might listen. Let them think it's a good idea. Let them bring her.

Not that I *wanted* April to see me like that. I clearly recalled the shame I'd felt, back in the city, when I'd callously thought of using her like a weapon, the way Manta had used me.

Still, seeing me wouldn't *do* anything to her, I thought, except terrify her a bit more. And if it didn't work, neither of us would be any worse off. But the plain fact was that her huge poltergeist power was the only hope for both of us, now.

And the last time she'd seen me bloody and battered and being viciously attacked, she'd destroyed a whole room in a museum.

*

The darkness gave me no clear idea how much time was passing, but I suppose it was morning when the red lights flicked on again. But to my surprise no one came down the steps to start torturing me again. Instead, two of the sorcerers, Dyer and Blist, came to stand on the gallery, followed by a few watchmen and servitors.

The two mages seemed on edge, with what looked like a mixture of excitement and anxiety, as if they were waiting for something. That stirred a tiny hope within me – and some curiosity too, as I listened to their talk.

'I still think we should *all* be upstairs helping Mr Redman,' the tubby Dyer said, almost pouting. 'It's no easy task, setting up spells to shield a place this size against a demonic power. Who knows what it could do if it broke through?'

'Mr Redman knows, that's who,' muttered the small grey one, Blist. 'And he doesn't need all of us to deal with a bodiless creature that's terrified of fire.'

Dyer grimaced. 'Viney will be so smug that he chose *her*.'

'Never mind,' Blist said wearily. 'This is more important work. If it wasn't, Fray would be up there too.'

In the midst of my anxiety, I was thinking hard. A bodiless creature afraid of fire? That described the misty winter-demon that I'd burned, the one Redman had called a Skryl.

It sounded as if another of the creatures was now threatening the Cartel.

I thought of Redman talking about the 'inconvenience' I'd caused them. And Fray snarling about the 'trouble' I'd caused by killing the Skryl.

Maybe now another winter-demon, blaming Redman and company for sending the first Skryl to its death, had arrived feeling vengeful.

But with Redman and Viney magically 'shielding' the house, as Dyer had said, I didn't think an angry Skryl was going to trouble them. And I knew, in the next moment, that it wasn't going to be any help to me.

Both sorcerers tensed, heads tilting as if listening to an unspoken message. Then they smiled evilly at one another, before turning the ugly smiles towards me.

'You know,' Dyer said thoughtfully, 'we could do something different, instead of just holding him up in the air. It might be even more effective if he were seen to be *bathed* in blood. Literally.'

Blist nodded, with a tiny smile. 'Excellent idea.'

So as the new day's work began, the stone slab didn't disappear from beneath me as it had before. Instead, its shape magically changed, so that its edges rose *around* me, turning it into something like a shallow bathtub.

Still unable to move my body, I lay there waiting to

find out what kind of new horror the two sorcerers were planning.

Then I heard the clicking and chittering, and saw what was crawling out of the walls.

33

They looked spidery, but they were bigger than any spiders. They also had more legs – long, thin, ending in claws – and wicked pincer jaws. And they were hungry.

They crawled over me, chittering and biting. And each bite tore away a bit of my skin and flesh. Slowly, the swarm of hell-bugs started to eat me alive.

At the same time the magic that had brought them was, oddly, also keeping them away from my face. And in the tiny part of my mind that wasn't focused on screaming I thought, hoped, that it was so that my face wouldn't be masked by blood.

So *someone* would be sure to recognize me.

But the rest of me just screamed, awash in my own blood just as Dyer had said, as it collected in the stone bath.

Fighting the pain so I wouldn't pass out, I saw the two sorcerers tear their gaze from me, turning to the doorway that led from the gallery, looking expectant.

A moment later, an object like a long bundle of white cloth came floating through the doorway. Followed by Fray, looking savagely eager.

The bundle drifted beyond the gallery rail and paused, hovering in the air. Then Fray moved a hand and the white shape rose upright as if pulled by invisible strings.

It wasn't a cloth bundle. It was April.

She looked a lot like she had when I saw her for the first time, when she'd been about to be sacrificed by those dark-magic maniacs. Pale and still, her long hair streaming down behind her, wrapped in a white gown – which was tinged with crimson in that light.

But this time she was awake, her eyes stretched wide with horror.

'Here is your friend, dear girl,' Fray said to her, his smile even hungrier. 'See what has been happening to him? And soon, when the spiderlings are removed and his changeless body has recovered, we're going to cut off bits of him. Fingers, toes, ears . . .'

I heard a snigger, and saw the vampire woman, Elg, coming on to the gallery behind April. April turned her head, flinched and looked even more horrified. Elg was carrying a large, bright cleaver.

'I wonder which parts will grow back first,' Fray mocked.

That made Elg snigger again, and the two sorcerers grinned as Fray went on, enjoying his moment.

'Don't you wish you could help him, my dear?' Fray sneered. 'But we have locked your powers away again, haven't we?' He bared small yellow teeth. 'And you will not regain them until you have become one of us!'

April flinched again, her face twisting as she floated above me. And despite my agonies I watched her in desperate hope. She looked horrified beyond bearing as she stared down at the helpless howling ruin that I was, in a welter of my own blood, smeared with filth, covered in evil bugs and the wounds they made.

Then her eyes glazed and her face crumpled as if it was all too much for her. As if the sight of me like that, not a longed-for rescuer but another victim, was crushing her spirit and overpowering her mind. Just as Fray wanted.

Hope dwindled within me. It looked as if the new blockage in her mind was too strong after all. Though she'd been able to get those aimless mental cries through to me, her wild violent PK wasn't breaking out this time.

In my anguish, in that final shattering desolate loss of hope, all I could do was gather what small scraps remained of my strength – and scream her name.

As my scream echoed around that cellar, her body

jerked and stiffened, her eyes rolled back so only the whites showed, a fleck of foam appeared on her lips.

It looked just like what I'd feared – that in the face of all these unbearable extra horrors, her mind had given way.

But that wasn't what had been broken.

'*Nick . . .*'

Not a shriek but a breathy whisper. Not from April's mind but from her mouth.

With it her eyes returned to normal. They were still wide and staring, still appalled. But I saw something else in them. Something new – and stronger than mere horror.

Fury.

Still floating in mid-air, she half turned her head towards the group on the gallery, who were only beginning to look startled, and smiled.

Combined with the look in her eyes, it was by far the most frightening smile I had ever seen.

Then the whole chamber exploded.

The gallery vanished in a hail of splinters. With no time to protect themselves, the sorcerers and the others were flung in all directions. I had a glimpse of Fray crashing to the floor, spreadeagled and broken like a squashed insect. I saw Elg slamming into the far wall, her pain-filled scream silenced when a long splintery piece of the gallery buried itself in her chest like a sword.

And I saw the whole enormous weight of the collapsing ceiling and walls come thundering down upon us all in a colossal avalanche of dust and stone.

34

Amazingly, I survived.

The crushing overthrow of the sorcerers broke their magical grip on me. And the eruption – or a kindly bit of April's power – flipped over the blood-filled bath, pinning me underneath. It held firm, protecting me as the masonry thundered down.

Dimly wishing that I could have watched the hell-bugs being squashed by the falling stone, I passed out again.

When I came to, my body was back to normal, pain-free. The half-buried bath had been lifted away from me, leaving me lying unharmed on the rubble-strewn floor. And I was more startled when I discovered that I was clean – no longer crusted with dried blood and filth – and wearing my jeans and shoes.

Staring around, I saw April, like an angel in her white gown, standing quite still in the midst of the dev-astation that looked like the aftermath of a bomb. When I went over to her, I saw that she was looking at what was left of Elg. Along with the shaft of wood that had impaled her, a big sharp-edged chunk of stone now lay where Elg's head had been.

'We have to move,' I said. 'Others will be coming . . .'

April turned to me, her expression calm. 'I don't think so. This is a big house, and this cellar is sound-proof. I can't sense anyone coming.'

That was good news. Certainly I couldn't hear anything. And the ruined cellar was totally silent. Nothing, not even one of the bugs, was stirring under the rubble.

'This was even better than the museum,' I said.

She nodded. 'And it was because of you, again. When you screamed like that, it felt like a huge door bursting open inside my head.' Her mouth curved in a small smile. 'And they were so sure they had totally blocked my PK.'

'I heard you call to me, with your mind,' I told her. 'And scream.'

'I screamed a lot,' she murmured. 'They were in my head. With nightmares, monstrosities . . .'

'I'm sorry,' I said. 'They found you because of me.'

'It's not your fault,' she said. 'They probably would have found me sooner or later. And I know that you went away to try to keep me and Paddy and Julia safe. Paddy knew that too.'

'Didn't work,' I muttered. 'There was a monster that

had trailed me to the house, and they must've been tracking it. So they spotted you . . .'

Her mouth trembled. 'It was horrible. Two of the mages came with some of their monsters, and just broke in, somehow getting past Paddy's protections. Luckily Julia was out, but Paddy had no chance. I saw flames all over the front of him . . . Then I was taken away.'

'I don't think Paddy's dead,' I told her. 'Fray said something about using you to find him.'

Her face shone like sunshine after rain. 'That's wonderful!' she breathed. Then her eyes grew fierce. 'And that won't happen now. They've *failed*. They did those terrible things to you, yet here you are without a scar. They tried to control my mind to make me their slave – but instead their evil *freed* my mind.'

'Everything?' I asked.

'No.' She sighed. 'My memories are all still buried, somehow, so I still can't remember anything before a year or so ago. I wish I could . . . But the psychic powers, the PK and ESP and everything – I can *control* that again. All of it.'

She turned her gaze on to a huge lump of stone, which leaped into the air and whirled in a circle before crashing down again.

I blinked, impressed. 'Is that how you cleaned me up and put clothes on me?'

'I found your clothes in a corner,' she said. 'Your coat and shirt were all torn up, so I left them.' Her mouth curved again. 'Don't be embarrassed. I did it as I lifted that stone thing off you, and I didn't look.'

I shrugged. 'I'm not embarrassed, just amazed.' Then a new thought struck me. 'Could your mind power find Fray in all this?'

She looked around, and several lumps of stone lifted away, nearby. 'There.'

When I got to him the mage looked dead, covered in blood, his legs smashed. But he groaned as I pulled him on to his side. Then I wrenched the knife and its sheath off him, and put the tip of the blade to his throat as he had done to me.

But he was unconscious, helpless, probably dying. And I couldn't finish him off in cold blood. Not even him.

So I fastened the sheath back on my hip, put the knife in it and turned away. And when I almost tripped over the body of a watchman, I had another idea. I undid his body-armour and tossed it aside, then pulled off his jacket. Another stolen leather jacket, slightly too big, to keep me warm.

Meanwhile April had used her power to heap broken stone into a ramp, so we could climb up to the door leading out of the chamber. The door took us to a dim corridor where we crept along nervously in the knife's glow. But when we came to a junction with a broader corridor we paused, not sure which way to turn.

'I think they brought me from that way,' April whispered, pointing to the right.

Then we froze. From the direction where she was pointing, we heard the sound we feared most.

Loud angry shouts, and the thud of running feet.

It had to be Redman and more of his people. Redman's magic had sensed, at last, what had happened in his cellar. We wouldn't be taking *him* by surprise.

We ran in a wild sprint, with April's power pulling down the ceiling and shattering the walls behind us to slow the pursuers down. But we could hear more rumbles and crashes, and I knew that Redman's power was flinging the rubble out of his way just as easily.

Soon we burst through a doorway into a huge room. A rich man's room, with tall windows and a high ceiling, a thick carpet and heavy furniture, a big warm fire in an elegant fireplace. It looked wonderful, like a dream of luxury. But the best part of it for us was the other door on the far side.

As we leaped towards it, I braced myself for what we might find beyond it. And as I reached for the handle, I found out.

The door burst open with a crash, flinging us back. Two watchmen charged in, guns in their hands. And behind them came the woman sorcerer, Viney, hysterical rage blazing in her eyes.

184

35

April sent the watchmen flying, to crash against the wall and slump to the floor. In the same instant Viney's magic struck us both like an invisible club, hurling April over a big table, throwing me almost into the fireplace.

As I started to get to my feet, still gripping the knife, Viney ignored me. Knowing where the real danger was, the woman lunged towards April.

At the same time, Viney stopped being human.

Her arms and hands stretched impossibly long, with spiky thorns sprouting from her skin, hooked claws growing from her fingertips. And every needle-point dripped with thick evil slime that I knew would be a deadly venom. Her neck extended as well, snakily, and her head narrowed, her mouth opening to show curved fangs also oozing poison.

And as the Viney-monster reached for April, the fanged jaws widening even more, I reached bare-handed into the fire, grabbed a blazing log and threw it.

April's PK probably helped my aim. The log went just where I wanted it – into the monstrous gape of those jaws.

Viney could only manage a thin choking squawk, with the fiery log jammed in her throat. Her claws jerked up, scrabbling at her mouth. I saw April's eyes glint as she gathered herself.

And Viney's grotesque head, burning log and all, exploded like a huge messy firework.

As the headless body toppled, April sprang to her feet. 'Come on,' she gasped. 'Let's go . . .'

But I didn't move. I was staring with horror at what was coming through the door where we'd come in.

'No,' Redman growled, his scarlet devil-face shiny in the firelight. 'You've gone rather too far already.'

April didn't flinch. Even as she whirled to face him, her power grasped most of the room's furniture and hurled it at him, a barrage of sofas, tables, lamps . . .

But it all simply swerved around and past him. Some of it flattened the watchmen who had come in with him. The rest smashed harmlessly into the wall.

'So your gifts have fully flowered at last,' Redman snarled. Like Viney had done, he was ignoring me, his furious glare fixed on April. 'But flowers can be plucked. A waste of a great potential – but a bearable loss.'

April tried again. Every remaining log in the fire-place leaped into the air and flew at him. But they were only halfway across the room when the flames went out and the logs turned to dry sawdust, fluttering uselessly to the floor.

I saw the fierce glitter in Redman's eyes, and knew that he was about to attack her. Ignoring my scorched hand, I hefted the knife and readied myself to leap at him.

And behind me a familiar gruff voice said, 'Move aside, son.'

I spun around, staring with disbelief. Paddy, as alive as ever, was striding through the doorway that Viney had blasted open. With Julia, looking scared but determined, behind him. And with a gleaming shotgun in his hands.

'Who in all the hells are *you*?' Redman roared.

Without replying, Paddy bared his teeth and aimed the shotgun. But Redman made a throwing motion, and a crimson stream of magical flame burst from his hand. It seemed to take a fanged dragon-shape as it blazed across the room. And it struck Paddy full in the chest.

The shotgun fired harmlessly into the ceiling as Paddy flew backwards, crashing into Julia and sending her flying as well. And Paddy's whole front became a mass of flame, no longer red but blindingly white-hot.

But as I yelled and April screamed, I saw – through the burnt ruin of Paddy's shirt and jacket – a disc of silvery metal with a crystal at its centre, somehow fixed to his chest. Paddy's amulet, still protecting him.

Shaken but unhurt, he raised the shotgun again. Beside him, poor thin Julia sprang up as if ready to leap at Redman bare-handed.

But the second blast from the shotgun swerved around Redman just as April's missiles had. And before anyone else could move, Redman spat a strange harsh word and swung a hand in a sweeping gesture.

The amulet had no effect against that. Paddy and Julia went flying across the room as if in the grip of a hurricane.

But before they struck the wall, they disappeared.

I heard April's choked cry as I started my leap. But Redman twitched his other hand, and his magic hurled us both with crushing force against the wall.

'You have caused much disturbance, and great inconvenience,' he snarled. 'But there was never any likelihood that you would escape. And the torments you both have suffered so far will seem *delights*, compared to what will happen to you now.'

With April lying in a heap, stunned, perhaps hurt, I struggled dazedly to find my feet. But I was still off-balance, leaning against the wall, when the whole room went weirdly dim and still and icy cold.

And even Redman seemed to be paralysed when, in

the air before him, a vertical line appeared, then spread into a hazy, quivering gap.

And sheer terror flowed through it.

36

It was a shadowy, dark-grey mass, tall and narrow. Not solid, but wavery and floaty like thick smoke. With two pale holes in its darkness like eyes. Though it was bigger and not ghostly-white, it made me think of the Skryl that I had fought.

And of the vengeful Skryl that Dyer and Blist had talked about.

Redman glowered at it, looking unafraid. 'How did *you* get in?' he demanded.

The smoky creature drew itself up even higher, looming over him. 'The fall of your helpers has brought down your paltry barriers,' it said, in a hollow tone like a voice from a tomb. 'Yet even without that, I would have found a way.'

'Then find your way out again,' Redman growled. 'While you still can.'

'I do not fear your threats, sorcerer.' The creature's misty shape was roiling like storm clouds. 'Do you take me for just another warrior? I am the Arch-Magister of the Caverns, in the Skryl realm. And I have come to demand payment.'

'Payment?' Redman repeated warily. 'What payment?'

The creature loomed closer to him. 'Your sorcery plucked a young Skryl warrior from our realm, imposed your will on him, forced him to serve your evil purpose. In that service he died – and now you will pay.'

Redman's scarlet face grew mottled, and rage burned in his shiny black eyes. His hands flickered, and two bursts of magical flame stormed through the air. But from the Skryl's grey shape flew two patches of cold smoky darkness that met the flames in mid-air and quenched them.

Snarling, Redman tried again. Tall bright tongues of fire sprang from the floor around the Skryl, enveloping him. But at once a cloud of ice crystals burst from the Skryl's cloudiness, turning the room briefly arctic, smothering the flames and leaving thick frost on the carpet.

'Struggle as you may, mage,' the Skryl intoned, 'I will prevail. And in my realm you will suffer for a thousand years.'

'Fool of a demon!' Redman roared. 'I didn't kill your warrior! *There* is his killer! Take *him*!'

And he raised a shaking finger and pointed at me.

The smoky creature swirled again. 'The boy fought

to defend himself against the warrior, as was his right. The fault is not his. *You*, sorcerer, brought the warrior here and sent him to his death. The debt is *yours*.'

It surged forward. Redman yelled again, his magic throwing up a sheet of fire in front of him, bringing another blazing torrent of flame down from the ceiling on to the Skryl. But the seething dark column flung out its ice crystals again, and every flame vanished beneath them.

Then Redman changed his strategy. With veins throbbing on his scarlet scalp he raised both hands, bellowed a stream of words that crackled and echoed in the air, and closed his fists.

And a mighty invisible power seemed to clamp itself on to the Skryl, halting him, holding him still, binding his icy powers.

'Now, Arch-Magister . . .' Redman snarled, baring his black shark-teeth. 'Now we can see who will prevail.'

He began to mutter more ugly inhuman words that scraped at my mind. I heard a low creaking groan from the Skryl as the magical power that gripped him seemed to tighten. Then Redman opened one fist – and a wide flat bowl appeared in that outstretched hand. It looked like dark gleaming stone or glass and seemed heavy, but Redman held it easily.

And I saw something like thick red-hot mud begin

to gather in the bowl, like the molten lava that burns in a volcano's heart.

The bowl grew larger, the bubbling, smoking sludge filling it to the top, flames dancing on its surface. And though the weight must have been immense, Redman's hand raised it easily, magically lifting it high.

His devil-face contorted with glee as the Skryl's groans became deep howls of desperation. Then Redman braced himself, carefully balancing the huge bowl as if to hurl the terrifying stuff at his enemy.

But in his concentration, and perhaps his usual confidence, he wasn't paying any attention to his other enemies.

April was still on the floor, unmoving, but I was on my feet. And I had no doubt that when Redman had dealt with the Skryl he'd turn on us again.

I didn't really have much to lose.

Knife in hand, I launched myself across the room. And Redman, fully focused on hurling the blazing mass of lava, didn't hear or see me until it was too late.

As the arm supporting the bowl began to move I swung the knife, and the golden blade bit deep into his wrist. He yelled in shock and pain, jerked away, then shrieked in far greater agony – because the movement had sent some of the red-hot lava splashing across his face and chest.

Still shrieking, he dropped the bowl, clawing with

both hands at the molten searing ooze that clung to him.

But the spell that had made the lava had been broken, and the bowl vanished. And so did the power that gripped the Skryl.

Freed, the tall pillar of darkness surged forward, pulsing and swelling. Before the screaming Redman could defend himself, its icy swirling form had wrapped itself around him.

Redman's screams were silenced and his struggles halted. Within the cloudy shape that gripped him I had a glimpse of his black-fanged mouth opening wide in a final silent howl as thick ice began to form on his crimson skin.

Then the Skryl Arch-Magister flowed back through the vertical gap in the air, with his captive, and disappeared.

37

Behind me I heard a choked gasp, and turned to see April getting to her feet, pale and wide-eyed. For a long moment we just looked at each other, wordless and dazed.

In that suddenly silent place of ruin and horror and death, we found ourselves free and unthreatened. And for that moment we were blankly unable to think of what we should do next.

Then April stirred, with a sigh that was almost a sob. 'What do you think he did to Paddy and Julia?' she whispered.

'I don't know.' I glanced at the knife in my hand, glad to see it glowing silver again, and sheathed it. 'But I'm going to try to find out.'

'He might have sent them to some demon place,' she said, her eyes dark.

I shook my head. 'I don't think so. Paddy once told me that reaching to a demon realm takes a lot of power and a big ritual. Redman just sort of moved his hand.'

'That's true,' she said, brightening. 'Maybe he only sent them somewhere else in this country.' She gave me a piercing look. 'And we're *both* going to find out.'

As I held her gaze, she smiled. Then we turned towards the door.

Outside, I was amazed to find that we'd been in a big, rambling, ordinary-looking house in an ordinary peaceful bit of countryside. As we walked unhurriedly away, the sun was bright on the fields and hedges, birds were singing, the air was cool and fresh. It was hard to believe that so much cruelty and monstrous evil had gone on in such a place.

'You know,' I said carefully, 'there's a chance that . . . that Paddy and Julia didn't survive.'

'We have to believe that they did,' April said, looking determined. 'And if we keep moving, travelling around, I might get a psychic sense of them, wherever they are. That's probably how Paddy managed to find us.'

'Sounds like a plan,' I said. 'I'd want to keep moving anyway. It's the way I've lived most of my life.' I glanced down at the ill-fitting jacket and my torn jeans, and at her white gown. 'First, though, any chance you might use your powers to find some clothes for us, and maybe some food?'

'I can try,' she said, then frowned. 'You know that Redman and his people were only a part of the Cartel.

The rest of it will come after us. And they *really* won't stop, now.'

'They've been after us for years,' I told her. 'We'll manage. You do the psychic stuff, and I'll do the survival stuff – and if we keep moving, like you said, we'll have a pretty good chance.'

'A very good chance,' she said, and her smile was like another sunrise. 'Maybe it's the Cartel that ought to start worrying.'

So we went on, side by side, across the soft turf of the field. And I thought about how interesting it would be, travelling with someone. Especially someone with a lot of power, who might be Manta's daughter, and who above all was an amazing and very special person.

It would be good to have her friendship and her company, during the search that had to be made.

It would be good not to be alone, when we came up against whatever lay ahead.

TORMENT

Douglas Hill

'He turned to watch me and smiled. A smile full of malice and cruelty . . . the terror was about to start again . . .'

Having defeated the sadistic Mr Redman, Nick must face the fact that he has put his only friends in deathly peril. Determined to save them, and with April by his side, he enters a netherworld of soulless suffering. A place where the mist hides a realm of nightmarish apparitions and where the path leads ever downwards into an eternity of pain . . .

THE INFINITY CODE

E. L. YOUNG

**Will Knight, 14: Inventive genius.
Creates cutting-edge gadgets (S.T.O.R.M.-sceptic)**

**Andrew Minkel, 14: Software millionaire
(and fashion disaster). Founder of S.T.O.R.M.**

**Gaia Carella, 14: Brilliant chemist with a habit of
blowing stuff up (usually schools).**

**Caspian Baraban, 14: Gifted astrophysicist.
Obsessed with the immense forces of space
(equally immense ego).**

Will mocks S.T.O.R.M.'s plan to combat global problems, but then they uncover a plot to create a revolutionary weapon. Will swallows his doubts as they race to Russia to confront the scientific psychopath with a deadly power at his fingertips.

The first book in the S.T.O.R.M. series, *The Infinity Code* is a gadget-packed high-adrenalin adventure.

A selected list of titles available from Macmillan Children's Books

The prices shown below are correct at the time of going to press. However, Macmillan Publishers reserves the right to show new retail prices on covers, which may differ from those previously advertised.

E. L. Young

S.T.O.R.M. – The Infinity Code	978-0-330-44640-2	£5.99
S.T.O.R.M. – The Ghostmaster	978-0-330-44641-9	£5.99
S.T.O.R.M. – The Black Sphere	978-0-330-44642-6	£5.99
S.T.O.R.M. – The Viper Club	978-0-330-45416-2	£5.99

Elizabeth Laird

Secrets of the Fearless	978-0-330-43466-9	£5.99
The Garbage King	978-0-330-41502-6	£4.99
A Little Piece of Ground	978-0-330-43743-1	£4.99

All Pan Macmillan titles can be ordered from our website, www.panmacmillan.com, or from your local bookshop and are also available by post from:

Bookpost, PO Box 29, Douglas, Isle of Man IM99 1BQ

Credit cards accepted. For details:
Telephone: 01624 677237
Fax: 01624 670923
Email: bookshop@enterprise.net
www.bookpost.co.uk

Free postage and packing in the United Kingdom